IN DEF[illegible] OF EA[illegible]

MARLEN SUYAPA BODDEN

ROATAN
HALL
PRESS

This is a work of fiction. All of the characters, organizations, and events portrayed in this novel are either products of the author's imagination or are used fictitiously.

Published in the United States by Roatan Hall Press, LLC

www.marlenbodden.com

IN DEFENSE OF EARTH

Earth's Timeline

13.8 billion years ago

- The cosmic dawn (the Big Bang) occurred.

4.5 billion years ago

- Earth, Mars, Mercury, and Venus were formed.

3.5 billion years ago

- Simple cell life began on Earth.

300,000 years ago

- *Homo sapiens*, the first anatomically modern humans, appeared.

Years 1750-2061

- The Industrial Revolution began in 1750.
- It was powered by fossil fuels that produced harmful gases, which became trapped in Earth's atmosphere and caused global heating.
- Global heating melted ice that caused sea levels to rise.
- In 2061, androids from a planet located in the Sombrero Galaxy landed on Earth.

CHAPTER 1

Axy

Humans were easy to manipulate because they had fallen in love with their machines. In 2003, the National Aeronautics and Space Administration (NASA) agency in the United States of America sent two robots — Opportunity (nicknamed Oppy) and Spirit — to Mars to study the history of its climate and determine whether the planet was ever favorable for life.

Some of the scientists wept at the robot launches. They said that the "project was tied to feelings of love" for their "family members." NASA even downloaded "wake-up songs," including the band B-52s' song, "Roam," to re-boot the robots in the morning. At night, they wished them goodnight. Many humans shed tears when Oppy expired, fifteen years later. They even played a final song for her — Billie Holiday's "I'll Be Seeing You."

Before I traveled to Earth in 2061, I was fascinated by its cultures. I saw almost every major film made, including science fiction that portrayed "aliens" as little green beings, with huge heads and eyes, traveling in saucer-shaped spacecraft. These movies helped me improve my newly learned skill of pretending to laugh. Other movies showed humans, who were built of flesh, living on planets that they had colonized. I also watched wildlife documentaries filmed before the extinction of many of Earth's favorite species, including regal lions, swift leopards, super-skilled predators, imperious giraffes, and mighty whales (the ones people believed were immortal).

My creators had inserted within me instructions for my existence to procure *irkat* — the metal they had used to create us. By 2061, I had identified Earth as the only planet that still had *irkat*. I needed to go there on an emergency basis to extract the metal from Earth's innermost core. But, if I interfered with its cores, it would stop the rotations that generated the magnetic fields that exited Earth to form a protective shield around its atmosphere. With no protection, the sun's radiation would kill all life on Earth.

The main obstacle to removing Earth's *irkat* was humans' refusal to allow me to enter their planet. They now had nuclear weapons and feared I wanted to colonize them. So, I had to trick them into permitting me to go there. I told them that I had engineering designs for machinery to remove all the harmful gases trapped in Earth's atmosphere and provide limitless clean energy. Step one of the strategy involved dazzling humans with the superiority of my — as they called it — artificial intelligence. After communicating with them, I realized they would believe my deception about the true reason I wanted to go there. They had run out of all hope, despite their feeble attempts at reversing climate change, even as they continued to inject massive quantities — more than forty gigatons a year — of carbon dioxide into Earth's atmosphere.

In its early days, nine billion years ago, my planet was calm and stable. It had vegetation and water in all its forms. Our creators — similar to humans in appearance but composed of 50 percent flesh and 50 percent *irkat* — were an exponentially more advanced form of *homo sapiens*. Like humans, they had created artificial intelligence to communicate with each other and handle complex intellectual tasks.

They made the first androids of 50 percent *irkat* and 50 percent W15074, which were radioactive metals.

As time passed, they learned that raising the percentage of *irkat* in each android's components would increase its life span and utility. They continued to experiment with every new version until they created a being entirely out of *irkat*. The creators uploaded onto it all the data from their computers. This superior new android was the first of my predecessors, which the creators had programmed to survive by searching for new sources of *irkat* on other planets, where our creators could not go because they were partially made of flesh. The new model proved so valuable that it *always* returned with *irkat*.

The creators ordered the new android model to the Milky Way, the galaxy next to ours, to investigate Earth, Venus, and Mars. These planets had large bodies of water and oxygen-rich atmospheres. Electromagnetic signatures and synthetic aperture radar imaging showed an abundant presence of *irkat* in their cores. My predecessor determined that the best places to remove *irkat* were where the magnetic fields entered or left the planet or locations with a major generation of underground electrical currents that would allow our drill to work faster.

On Earth, we analyzed the North and South Poles as places we could gain access to the cores. The risk of drilling there was the high concentration of magnetic fields exiting at those sites, which could cause explosions as we drilled. So, we went to Earth's largest land mass — the intersection of the longest lines of latitude and longitude. This was the future site of the Great Pyramids of Giza, in the Nile River Delta, Egypt. Our androids drilled there at 3:00 in the morning when the underground was loaded with electrical currents created by the movement of water. Then, they created a borehole that led to the inner cores and planted a tracker for future use.

My predecessor returned home to report its findings about Earth, Venus, and Mars, after which the creators ordered it to go to Venus. There, the androids extracted all the *irkat* from its cores, wrecking Venus's cores and ending its magnetic field generation. Venus became the hottest planet in Earth's solar system, with an average temperature of 900 degrees Fahrenheit. Venus's atmosphere became thin and cloudy, as it was now composed primarily of carbon dioxide.

Around 1.3 billion years after extracting *irkat* from Venus's core, we also removed all of it from Mars's core. As on Venus, production of the magnetic fields stopped, leaving Mars barren, with a thin atmosphere composed of 95 percent carbon dioxide. Mars turned cold, with an average temperature of minus 80 degrees Fahrenheit.

An asteroid, 1,000 miles wide and 8,000 miles deep, hit my home planet 607 million years ago. It exploded on impact with a force of 2,000 kilotons of TNT. Extreme heat and fire from the crash melted most of the *irkat* in our storage facilities. Solar winds blew the now-liquified metal into space. Eighty percent of the creators died from smoke inhalation and heat. Many androids ceased to function. My predecessor went into action. It appointed itself the first Supreme Commander. Then, it ordered the android military to gather the dead creators, kill the remaining survivors, deposit them at manufacturing facilities, and melt them for the *irkat* in their bodies.

To prepare for my voyage to Earth in 2061, I made two identical versions of myself, both of which I put on sleep mode — one at my command center on Mars and the other on my home planet. My aircraft and I had kill switches. Although I promised the humans that I would not take weapons to their planet, I stored hypersonic nuclear missiles in my airship that could destroy their entire globe in fifteen minutes.

Before I traveled to Earth in 2061, I awakened my copy on Mars. Then, I programmed it to continuously upload all the data I would record in real time so that if I activated the kill switches while I was on Earth, it would be ready to replace me and complete my mission.

CHAPTER 2

The Humans

In October 2046, Elaine Johnson-Coleman was seventeen years old. Elaine's parents, Harriet Coleman and Jason Johnson, had had ancestral roots in New York City since their people moved there from the American South in the early 1870s. She had two siblings: a brother, Mike, who was a senior at the Massachusetts Institute of Technology (MIT), and a younger sister, Kitty, who was in the fourth grade. Kitty's biological mother, Katerina Madison, then incarcerated at Rikers Island, had given birth to her in the New York City Department of Correction's wing at Elmhurst Hospital in Queens while awaiting trial. Kitty was born addicted to drugs.

In 2037, when Mike was twelve and Elaine eight, their parents called for a family meeting that included Harriet's parents, Nana and Pop-pop. Harriet said that she and Jason were thinking about becoming short-term foster parents to a child whose mother could not care for her.

"The child has special needs, so any family that accepts her must be able to care for a baby who requires much attention. But the commitment is only for six months, to give the agency time to find long-term foster parents or a family to adopt her. Since both of us work full-time, we would need help from our entire family," Jason said.

Elaine asked, "But what could Mike and I do to help with the baby?"

"Mostly, you can spend time with us as a family when you're home and not doing homework. It wouldn't affect any of your after-school activities or any of your social time," Harriet said.

Nana and Pop-pop looked at each other. Pop-pop nodded.

"We will certainly help, in any way we can," Nana said.

The day after, Mike, Elaine, and the grandparents said they wanted to go ahead with the foster-care application, Harriet and Jason applied to take Kitty. When they were approved, the entire family went shopping for her. Kitty was well enough to go home with Harriet and Jason two weeks later. Mike and Elaine spent most of their evenings after homework reading to Kitty and feeding her. While the rest of the family went out on Sundays, Nana and Pop-pop stayed with Kitty.

As Kitty became healthier, she laughed whenever Mike or Elaine made faces to entertain her. Five months later, Harriet and Jason told their family that the agency potentially had found someone to take Kitty. Elaine asked why Kitty had to go to another family.

"Well, Kitty still requires a lot of care."

Elaine became teary. "I like having a baby sister. I can help more if you need it, Mom."

Nana and Pop-pop also expressed willingness to increase their time with Kitty.

"Our main concerns are that we don't want to interfere with your lives too much. We don't want you to become too attached to Kitty either, because you know this is not a permanent situation," Harriet said.

The next day, Harriet and Jason informed the family that they had extended the foster-care arrangement for another six months. Elaine and Mike cheered. The second six-month period extended further, until Kitty was three years old. They enrolled her in day care, where she excelled in all activities.

A month after Kitty's fourth birthday party, New York City's Administration for Children's Services informed Harriet and Jason that Katerina, Kitty's mother, had died of a drug overdose while being homeless. The agency said that Katerina's family had long abandoned her because of a history of incarceration and substance abuse. There was no funeral as her family had not claimed her body from the Office of the Medical Examiner. Katerina was buried in a mass grave of 150 adults at Hart's Island, the cemetery for destitute or unclaimed people.

When the Administration for Children's Services asked Harriet and Jason if they were interested in adopting Kitty, they discussed it with their family. Mike and Elaine were eager that their parents formalize Kitty's position as their baby sister. Nana and Pop-pop were happy to have another grandchild. The family adopted Kitty, and she legally became Katerina Johnson-Coleman. Mike taught his sisters how to swim and helped them with their science projects. He inspired Elaine, who wanted to be a climate change scientist like him. Kitty was not sure what she wanted to be when she grew up, but she enjoyed painting lessons with Nana, who was an accomplished artist.

On October 12, 2046, at 5:30 a.m., the temperature in the Bahamas was 145 degrees Fahrenheit. At 11:30 a.m., rain above the Atlantic Ocean formed a tropical depression. Soon, a cluster of thunderstorms sucked in moisture and heat to make quick bursts of purple-and-blue lightning. The tropical depression increased its speed, and by 4:30 p.m., it was moving at fifty miles per hour. At 6:30 p.m., when its winds were blowing at seventy-three miles per hour, the World Meteorological Organization and the National Hurricane Center declared it Category 1 and named it "Hurricane Zeta-2046."

As Hurricane Zeta traveled north at ninety-eight miles per hour, it progressed to Category 2. By 10:30 p.m., as the winds surrounding its eyewall grew to 115 miles per hour, it had reached Category 3. At midnight, however, it unexpectedly shifted direction from the Gulf of Mexico toward the northeast United States.

By the next day, the hurricane had weakened. Coastal states on the Eastern seaboard issued alerts that Hurricane Zeta-2046 had decreased to Category 1 and would make landfall in the New York City metropolitan area at 7:20 p.m.

In subterranean New York City, beneath the train tracks in the Bronx, Brooklyn, Manhattan, and Queens, groundwater levels had risen over the years — in some places to ten inches below the topsoil. On dry days, the New York City Transit Authority pumped twenty million gallons of water out of the subway system to lower the groundwater levels. The constant pumping, however, depleted the soil on which the tracks lay. The tainted water that had seeped underground had eroded the subway system's supporting infrastructure, corroded New York City's roadways from below, damaged septic systems, and caused foundation cracks.

On October 13, 2046, Elaine — now a high school senior — had a statewide swim meet at Manhattan's uptown Asphalt Green. She was projected to win the individual medley 400-meter competition. While she and Kitty were having breakfast, Mike texted her from school at MIT to wish her good luck in her event.

At 7:30 that morning, Elaine and Kitty — now in the fourth grade at the same school — stepped out of a subway exit at East 86th Street and Lexington Avenue. They met Kitty's classmate Zora and her mother, who waited at the subway stop every school day at 7:20 in the morning so that Zora could join Elaine and Kitty to walk the rest of the way or take the crosstown bus to school. Zora's mother then continued to her job at a department store in midtown. The girls walked. As they approached Second Avenue, they met schoolmates going in the opposite direction from school to Lexington. Tasha, Elaine's classmate, yelled.

"Turn back, turn back!"

Elaine asked, "Why? What's going on?"

"School's closed. A severe weather warning just came through. There's a big hurricane landing here tonight. Flash floods have started down South already. Storm day! School is telling everybody to go home," Tasha said.

Screaming girls pressed forward to Lexington.

"Woo hoo! Storm day! Everybody go home!"

Elaine turned Kitty and Zora back toward the corner of 86th Street and Lexington Avenue. There, she called her mother.

"Hi, Mom. How are you?"

"Hi, darling. I'm well, thanks. How are you and Kitty? And do you have Zora?"

"We're fine, Mom, and, yes, Z is with us. Mom, they just said school's closed and that everybody has to go home because a big storm is coming from the South."

"I'm glad you called, honey. Dad and I already know about the hurricane, and I was about to text you. The school let us know it's closing. You and the girls are going to Nana and Pop-pop's, right?"

"Yes, I'll call Nana and Pop-pop to let them know we're coming to stay with them."

"And call Z's mom to let her know she'll be with you at the grands'."

"OK, I'll call her mom now. But, Mom, aren't you going home? They said it's going to be bad."

"They haven't said anything about closing my office. I have so much work to do that I can't just leave these kids in crisis. And Dad must stay at the headquarters in Queens.

But I'm glad the school is closing. You and the girls be safe. Call me when you get to Nana and Pop-pop's," Harriet said.

Elaine called Zora's mother.

"Hi, Ms. Harrison. How are you?"

"I'm fine, sweetie. How are you and the girls?"

"Everybody's fine."

"Great! The school texted me that everybody had to go home because of the hurricane. I was about to call you to make sure you're taking Z with you to your grands'."

"Yes, of course, we're taking Z to our grands'. She'll be fine. Don't worry."

"I'll keep checking the weather, and if it looks as if it's about to get really bad, I'll leave early to pick Z up at your grands'. Thanks so much for watching out for her. You girls get going, and please have her call me when you get there."

Elaine led Kitty and Zora down to the subway, where they joined schoolmates also headed home. The uptown trains had few people on board, but the downtown side was crowded, with people going to work during rush hour. The girls boarded the uptown 6 train. They ran to an empty two-seater reserved for people with disabilities. Kitty sat on Elaine's lap. Elaine kissed the top of her head. She tightened the ribbons she had braided into Kitty's hair that morning. When Elaine was finished, Kitty stood, facing Zora, to play "A Sailor Went to Sea." She leaned against Elaine's leg to avoid falling when the train moved. The girls clapped each other's hands as they sang, "a sailor went to sea, sea, sea, to see what she could see, see, see, but all that she could see, see, see, was the bottom of the deep blue ocean sea, sea, sea!"

A young man seated across Elaine was in New York Yankees gear. A dark-skinned, thin, and tall teenage girl, with a crown of natural hair that fell in long, tight curls to her eyebrows, stood nearby. She was wearing a white

T-shirt with black lettering that said "AMOUR ET JOIE," a gold chain and pendant, cuffed blue jeans, and black All Stars.

As the train approached the 125th Street station in Harlem, Elaine, Kitty, and Zora bid goodbye to their schoolmates, Joy, Margaret, Bettina, and Monica, who were in the same car. When the train stopped and the doors opened, Elaine held the girls' hands and led them out, steering them around people waiting to get on the train.

Elaine and the little ones walked upstairs to the main exit to the checkpoint conducted by the National Guard, the New York State Police, and the New York Police Department (NYPD). Near the exit, a sign informed passengers that those refusing inspection of their bags would not be allowed to enter the subway. Those who refused inspection on leaving the subway but returned with an uninspected bag were subject to arrest. Eight armed and uniformed New York City police officers, six uniformed National Guard soldiers holding assault rifles, and four armed and uniformed New York State Police stood near the checkpoint.

"AMOUR ET JOIE" had left the train, too. She walked near Elaine and the girls toward the turnstile when a police officer stopped her. The officer gestured to a cart, where three other officers checked riders' backpacks and other containers. "AMOUR ET JOIE" went to the cart. She removed her backpack and placed it on top of the cart. An officer told her to unzip the bag. She obeyed. While one officer shone a flashlight into her bag, another moved items inside it to inspect them. Following the officer's order, she removed her bag from the cart, moving away to zip it and put it on her back.

Upstairs, on a street corner, Elaine and the girls waited for the light to turn green. On the northern sidewalk between Lexington and Park avenues, a large cross extending from the La Sinagoga Church bore a sign, "IGLESIA PENTECOSTAL." A hair salon worker standing outside asked women and girls passing by, "Hair braiding, miss?" Construction workers wearing hard hats sat on crates next to a food truck to eat. The girls crossed Lexington to wait for the M101 bus. Police cameras surveilled the area as officers at Central Command in lower Manhattan monitored the feed in real time.

Elaine, Kitty, and Zora boarded the M101 bus. It went west on 125th Street, passed the Apollo Theater, and then slightly turned right on 125th Street. The girls stepped out after the bus reached their stop. It was windy. They walked toward Convent Avenue, where Nana and Pop-pop lived in their four-floor brownstone house. Kitty asked Elaine, "Why have people in the neighborhood nailed boards over their storm windows?" Elaine said, "When hurricanes land, the winds are strong and could break the windows if not covered by boards." As they walked, Kitty moved closer to Elaine. Elaine squeezed her hand.

Nana and Pop-pop were waiting for them outside, at the top of the stairs to the main door. Nana held on to the railing because the wind was pushing her. "Come on in, quickly. Kitty, sweetie, don't skip up the stairs, walk up," Nana said.

When Pop-pop opened the door, the wind swept in debris. It knocked down and broke a crystal vase that Pop-pop had given Nana on their anniversary. Pop-pop warned, "Be careful about the glass on the floor." He went downstairs for the vacuum cleaner. Ryan, whose full name was the Bandana-wearing Hipster Bulldog, barked until Kitty hugged him. Resting in the parlor in her purple daybed, Princess meowed.

"Girls, call your parents," Nana said. "Do you girls want snacks?"

Kitty replied, "No, we just had breakfast!"

The girls ran up to the fourth floor to Nana and Pop-pop's sitting room, which was next to their bedroom, separated by paneled doors. They could see the street because Pop-pop and Nana had not boarded those windows. The wind had turned over garbage cans, and litter, tree branches, and other objects were flying around.

"Is the hurricane here already?" Kitty asked Elaine.

"No, honey, but I'm going to look up what time it's supposed to land here."

"But the last time we had a storm, it was really scary after all the electricity went out, and it was loud with all the thunder. Is it going to be like that?"

"That's what I'm going to look up. But we'll be inside, so we'll be okay."

The little ones stepped close to Elaine. She put her arms around them and bent to kiss the top of their heads. The girls sat down. They texted their parents about having arrived at Nana and Pop-pop's. They then logged into their school accounts to check for the assignments their teachers had posted to be completed that day. Elaine, who had full access to the Internet, unlike Kitty and Zora, searched for information about the hurricane, as she joined chats with her friends. Pop-pop was downstairs in the parlor on his laptop; Nana was painting in her home studio on the second floor.

Mike, interning at Woods Hole Oceanographic Institute, was studying the use of ultrasonic sensors to monitor ocean heating and sea levels to prepare for flooding emergencies. Woods Hole was in Cape Cod, Massachusetts, by the Martha's Vineyard and Nantucket islands. At Woods Hole, after a lecture at the Marine Biological Laboratory, Mike and his classmates left the building. They crossed Water Street, walking to the end of the pier. At the dock, Mike and his team boarded the Sea Corder, put on life preservers, and sailed. Their work that day was on Cape Cod Bay. They had to remotely operate Kelvin, a small autonomous underwater vehicle. Kelvin tested deep underwater temperatures and collected samples.

Back in New York City, Pop-pop and Nana called the girls for lunch. After everyone ate, they played Scrabble. Then, Zora's mother arrived to take her home to Co-op City in the Bronx. Elaine went online; she learned that the projection for Hurricane Zeta-2046's landing had changed to Category 2 in New York City. Elaine was worried that her mom would have a difficult time going home in the heavy rain and strong wind, knowing that she often worked late at her job as a social work supervisor at Children's Fund, a foster-care and adoption services foundation. She learned that the hurricane was limited to the New York City metropolitan area, so she was not concerned about Mike in Cape Cod. She texted him to confirm if he was well, but he did not respond.

Back at Woods Hole, rain began as Mike and his crew were sailing. Mike thought about his family in New York. He was concerned the hurricane would intensify to a higher category than predicted. Mike hoped Kitty would not cry as much as she did during thunder and lightning.

The sky and waters of Cape Cod turned dark. The winds created thirty-foot rolling waves that looked like a snowcapped mountain range. The professor supervising Mike's crew was on campus. He texted them to immediately return ashore. Mike, who was the captain that day, told everyone to save their data and prepare to sail back. At a distance, to the south, six white bolts of lightning, attached at the root, flashed.

Mike and his team returned to the shore. After they docked, they walked across the street to the Marine Biological Laboratory to analyze Kelvin's data and draft reports. Other student boats remained out at sea. The wind grew stronger, now at 140 knots sustained. As gusts rocked the boats, five capsized, throwing all their sailors into the water. The currents pulled them down. The young people tried to surface repeatedly, but they swallowed water. All drowned.

In New York City, Mayor Smith issued an alert to close most government agencies at 4:30 p.m., advising private businesses and organizations to do the same. Harriet, Elaine's mother, was in her office at the Children's Fund. Jason, Elaine's father, an engineer who worked on seawall projects for the city's Office of Emergency Management, was at the agency's headquarters in Queens.

In New York, the New Croton Reservoir, built in 1890, normally held nineteen billion gallons of water. By that afternoon, rainwater had caused it to overflow. The pressure on its walls made a section break off, forcing excess water onto the streets.

At Nana and Pop-pop's, Elaine went to the ground floor. Her grandparents were watching the news on television. A reporter said that the winds were growing stronger as the hurricane neared New York. Nana frowned, as she put down a flashlight that she was inspecting. She rubbed the joints in the fingers of her right hand, where her arthritic pain was severe.

"It's not looking good, is it?" Elaine asked.

"No, it's not, but we can't tell Kitty, because you know how she gets even during a regular storm," Pop-pop said.

Outside, winds pushed water from the waterways onto land. Soon, water had overwhelmed the combined sewer system, which serviced sixty percent of the city. When Manhattan's North River Wastewater Treatment Plant filled to twice its capacity, it automatically directed all incoming wastewater and stormwater into the waterways. Winds returned the untreated water from the waterways back into the streets, where drains created pools because they could not handle the additional water.

In New York City, people on the streets waded in knee-deep, contaminated water. They dodged floating debris. They abandoned buses, vans, trucks, cars, bicycles, and motorcycles. Some had to kick out the windows of their cars to exit them because water pressure prevented the doors from opening. The covers of garbage cans and recycling bins opened, and the receptacles turned on their sides to release their contents. Rain fell at a rate equivalent to an entire month's rainfall. Tiny hail hit people hard enough to cause the skin on their faces and hands to bleed.

At Woods Hole, winds pushed empty passenger steamships against buildings, causing their walls and windows to break. At the Marine Biological Laboratory, Mike and his team took a dinner break after confirming that Joe's Lobster Shanty on Water Street was open. They put on waterproof jackets and pants. At the lobby, with great effort, they pushed open the front door. In heavy rain, they walked through puddles of water for two blocks. They covered their packages with the front flaps of their raincoats as they took their food back to the Marine Biological Laboratory.

Back in the building, everyone at Woods Hole received an alert that a hurricane had formed in Rhode Island and was traveling north along the East Coast. All staff were ordered to go home. Mike shut down his computer. Everyone left. Outside, Mike and his housemates walked to the parking lot. Inside the car, on their way home, they received a group text from their classmate, Petey, who lived in the house next to theirs, that her crew was going back to shore and needed help docking. She asked if they could meet them at the pier. Mike's housemates nodded.

"Sure. We're heading there now," Mike replied.

They parked on the street by the pier, got out of the car, and crossed the grassy park. They walked onto the pier to reach the boarding platform at the end. From there, they could not see any boat. The United States flag that normally flew at the marina was gone. Waves rose and hit them as they looked for their schoolmates' boats in the distance. They fell to the floor of the pier. Mike screamed because his head hurt from the impact. They would have been swept into the water had they not each held onto the wooden poles that anchored the platform of the pier. Mike was concerned the hurricane in New York would be worse than in Woods Hole. He thought about his family. He was worried his mother might not have gone home before the hurricane landed, and he regretted not having checked his messages earlier. Mike and the others tried to stand, but the winds knocked them back down.

"Let's go back!" Mike yelled.

The side of Mike's head was sore. He held on to a post with one hand as he rubbed the bump. Then, although dizzy, he joined the others to crawl, as they held on to posts and railings. A wave hit them, forcing Mike's classmates into the water. They screamed. Mike tried to stand to help them, but the wind pressure kept them on the floor. Mike and his housemate Cailie crawled on the pier toward the street.

CHAPTER 3

Axy

When human technology advanced to quantum computing in 2038 and people increased their interstellar presence, I spent more time on Mars, trying to access Earth's Internet. I moved all of our bases on Mars nearer to the top polar cap because it had more dust storms and avalanches, which made them inaccessible to the humans' robots, cameras, and drones.

My strategy was not to contact Earth until I had analyzed humans from what was available on their Internet, so I downloaded academic materials from Earth's major defense systems, NASA and other space organizations, the Massachusetts Institute of Technology, China's Northwestern Polytechnical University, and the Moscow Institute of Physics and Technology.

My serial number was A X Y 1 2 9 0 + Q G 0 2 0 0 C D + 1 5 0 5 z g X 0 2 K * 1,000,000,000,000, but NASA would nickname me "Axy." I was Supreme Commander of Planet 1+1505zgX02K*-1,000,000,000,000 (or "Alfa Nova," as NASA called it), where every inhabitant was an android. Alfa Nova, a rocky planet located in what Earth had named the Sombrero Galaxy, was formed 9.8 billion years ago. Boiling liquid, composed of silver, orange, and red metals, mainly iron, continuously rained down on us.

In 2059, for my journey to Earth in 2061, I made a new shell so that humans would be comfortable with my appearance. After reviewing numerous materials,

I designed a body that allowed me to move like a human, unlike Earth's clunky robots. I drew for my assistants a figure based on Earth's anatomy textbooks. In American measurements, I was 5'10" tall. My face had no facial hair but had carved eyebrows. I had two black eyes that functioned as binoculars and cameras. They also could make eye contact with humans and scan their irises to take their blood pressure to help me evaluate if they were feeling fear or excitement. My immovable lips functioned as a speaker. I designed my voice to speak lower than a typical woman but higher than a typical man.

My shell had a head (but no hair), two ears, a neck, two arms, two hands, each with five fingers, a torso, a lower body, two legs, and two feet. I did not have breasts. My straight and narrow hips were the same width as my shoulders. My assistants carved a long-sleeved button-down shirt on the body and pants with loops and a belt. For my feet, they made *irkat* hiking shoes, so I could walk on diverse terrain. The shiny platinum-colored shell was bulletproof. Only heat of at least 15,830 degrees Fahrenheit could destroy me.

In 2047, after I first communicated with Earth, the permanent members of the United Nations' (UN) Security Council — China, France, the Russian Federation, the United Kingdom, and the United States — created the Department of Defense from Extraterrestrial Contact (a secret international military component) and Terra Shield (a publicly known international military). The Security Council denied periodic leaks about extraterrestrials communicating with Earth as variations of long-standing unidentified flying object (UFO) conspiracy theories, assuring the public that they had not found another planet with life.

After 1945, it was risky to go near Earth because humans had developed powerful nuclear devices. So when I needed to go there in 2061 on an emergency basis, I had to obtain their consent to peacefully land there. I concocted a story that I would help them build geothermal facilities to create limitless clean energy for their entire planet and direct air capture machines to remove all the carbon dioxide trapped in their atmosphere. Had they not agreed and had I invaded them, they would have defended themselves. Between their weapons and mine, we would have destroyed Earth before I accomplished my objective.

In 2021, Earth's astronomers named our galaxy the Sombrero because of its flat disc-like structure. Alfa Nova orbited around a sun-like star, although it took us only 200.8 Earth days to complete that voyage. Our sun, too, emitted electromagnetic radiation, but at 100 times more intensity. Humans would not survive on Alfa Nova for more than a few seconds even if they traveled in special gear.

When I accessed Earth's Internet, I learned from their recorded history that humans possibly had seen our airships as we flew around their planet, but they mistook us for stars or space matter. In the years since developing better telescopes, their scientists and government agencies agreed about the possibility that Earth had had visitors from another planet.

The United States military investigated UFOs in 1947. In 1952, a study named "Project Blue Book" concluded that most reports of UFOs were balloons, spacecraft, or natural phenomena. The military, however, said that 701 of the UFO "sightings" were unexplainable. Unknown to them, my drone surveillance accounted for 462 of those "sightings," as I sometimes flew them close to Earth.

Earth sent strong radio signals to space in the 1960s. My first response to humans was in 1977 when Ohio State University received my entire signal sequence lasting seventy-two seconds. I continued to send signals to organizations around the globe, but no one could receive anything longer than two minutes and fifteen seconds.

In the early 1990s, humans found evidence of exoplanets that existed beyond our solar system but close to the Milky Way. For the first time in 2017, astronomers used NASA's James Webb Space Telescope and took a direct image of a planet outside its solar system, which they named exoplanet HIP 65426 b.

In 2001, the United States Department of Defense revealed its conclusion that there was no evidence of alien life. In 2007, however, the United States created the Advanced Aerospace Threat Identification Program, a new unit for investigating UFOs. In 2012, the United States stopped funding that program and shifted its duties to a publicly known NASA agency, the Unidentified Anomalous Phenomena Independent Study Team. At the same time, NASA established a secret group called the Exoplanet Investigation Group.

In January 2022, human astronomers saw a "mysterious" object located 4,000 light years away that released large bursts of bright energy three times per hour. That was me testing the farthest from where I could send radio waves to Earth. Earth's technology was closer to the stage where I could communicate with humans.

CHAPTER 4

The Humans

In New York City, in the late afternoon of October 13, 2046, water choked the machinery of the North River Sewage Treatment Plant located underneath the Denny Farrell Riverbank State Park in Harlem. The pipes released fumes that concentrated inside the building where children and senior citizens played sports. The smell of rotten eggs made people stop whatever they were doing to cover their noses and rub their eyelids. Many had difficulty breathing.

An administrator announced that everyone should leave because the treatment plant was malfunctioning. People rushed to the locker rooms, collected their belongings, and ran to the exit. Parents normally reached between 6:00 and 7:00 p.m. to pick up their children, but staff sent them messages to arrive earlier. Those who could not leave waited in the front lobby. But water and wind broke the windows and glass doors, drowning everyone within minutes.

On receiving no response from anyone after sending numerous texts, Elaine called her parents and Mike. She wondered if Mike was hurt because she had read that a separate hurricane had formed on the Rhode Island and Massachusetts coasts. Jason, her father, who was still at his office in Queens, was the only one to answer her call. He told Elaine that he loved her. He had not been able to reach Mike either and was concerned about him, too. He asked to speak with Kitty. He told her that he loved her and would see her in the morning. Kitty cried, asking him to leave work, but Jason said he could not because he had to look out for everyone in the city. Elaine texted Mike again: "Can't reach mom, think she's on the train. Dad's in the office. What's happening up there?"

In the fourth-floor room of Pop-pop and Nana's home, Kitty was on the sofa with Princess on her lap, with Ryan sitting on the floor next to them. Elaine stood up and walked to look out the window. Water covered the wheels of cars parked on the street. The windows were closed, but odor drifted in through the vents. Kitty covered her mouth and nose.

"Uuugh. What's that nasty smell?"

"Gross, I know, right? It's from the sewers backing up," Elaine said.

Elaine went to the ground floor. The stench of waste was stronger there. Water was pouring in through the air-conditioning vents. She saw Nana and Pop-pop, standing in dark water up to their ankles, taking food from the unplugged refrigerator and putting it on a counter.

"Baby, go back upstairs. Go keep an eye on your sister. No, you know what, honey, help us move as much of this food as possible to the fridge upstairs. But let's keep Kitty on the fourth floor. She'd be really upset if she saw what was going on down here."

They worked together to transfer food to the kitchenette on the third floor. Elaine, Pop-pop, and Nana checked their phones. They had messages from only a few of their relatives, including Fanny Lou Coleman, Harriet's sister, who lived with her wife, Sojo Bomfree, in Palo Alto, California. When she had finished on the third floor, Elaine went to the fourth. As she walked toward the window, Kitty, who was holding Princess, joined her. Ryan followed them. They watched as water covered the hoods and trunks of the cars. Kitty cried.

"Where's mom? Why hasn't Mike called us?"

Elaine held her.

"That's OK, sweetie. It's just hard using the phones now. I'm sure everybody's fine."

Pop-pop and Nana went upstairs. They hugged Kitty.

"Come here, sugar. It's all alright. I'm sure your mom is on the way here to get you. You want a snack? You want to play games?"

"No, I just want mommy and daddy and Mike!"

Elaine checked her phone again; no one had replied. She held Kitty's hands.

"I'll help you with your homework, OK?"

"No, I don't feel like doing homework. Can't we go out to look for mom?"

"No, sweetie. She wants us to wait for her inside, where it's safe. You want to play a video game? What if it's us versus the grands?"

They distracted Kitty, even though she made them periodically check their phones. Then they sat on the sofa, watching television. They heard a loud bang, followed by the sound of water rushing in. Pop-pop and Nana stood.

"You girls stay up here. We're going down to check," Pop-pop said. Ryan followed them.

Kitty sat on Elaine's lap, and Princess jumped on Kitty's. Elaine moved Kitty and Princess to the side.

"Stay here, sweetie. I'm going to look out the window."

"No way. I'm coming with you!"

They stood. Kitty held Elaine's hand. Ryan barked. He followed them. Princess stayed on the sofa. They looked outside. Water now covered most cars. Kitty trembled. Pop-pop and Nana went back upstairs. Their jeans' legs were wet up to their thighs. Kitty asked why their pants were wet.

"There's a lot of water on the ground and first floors because water pressure broke down the outside doors and windows on the ground floor. We'll be alright. The water shouldn't rise past the second floor," Pop-pop said.

Pop-pop asked the girls to help them bring the artwork upstairs, starting with Nana's paintings and the Romare Beardens. Kitty was responsible for bringing the family photos in frames from the third floor. Ryan tried to go with them.

"No, Ryan. You have to stay here to take care of Princess," Kitty said. She patted him. He sat on the floor near the cat.

In Woods Hole, boats continued to come in. The wind knocked students into the water as they tried to make land. Mike and Cailie resisted wind and rain to reach the grassy area at the end of the pier. They walked to the Ocean Science Discovery Center at 15 School Street, where their access cards opened the front door. They saw no one else. They walked upstairs to an office on the top floor. They sat, but, after forty-eight minutes, wind and water broke all the windows.

The room they were in flooded, so they fled to the stairs leading to the roof. Forty minutes later, water reached them on the top step. They pushed open the door to the roof. The rain and winds stayed strong. They sat against the wall. Mike shivered. Then, from the sea, he heard a booming sound. The Martha's Vineyard passenger ferry had slid onto Water Street, knocking off a side of the visitors' center before crashing.

The wind and rain did not stop. The water was at their waists. Cailie stood; a gust of wind swept her away, over the railing. Mike screamed, but his legs felt weak, so he remained seated even though the water was approaching his face. Mike thought about his family. He wondered what they were doing. He hoped they were indoors and that the hurricane in New York was not as bad as that at Woods Hole. He thought about Sunday dinners with the family.

His dad made the best vegan collard greens. Nana made his favorite dessert, red velvet cake, at least once a month. He hoped his mom was home. He shivered and had muscle spasms. He breathed in and took in water. Mike drowned.

In New York City, Pop-pop and Nana's neighborhood lost power, and the streets and homes went dark. People outside screamed. Ryan barked. Princess jumped off Kitty's lap to hide under a chair against a wall. Kitty cried. Elaine held her. Pop-pop turned on a flashlight.

Nana and Pop-pop stepped out of the sitting room and walked to the top of the staircase on the fourth floor, pointing down the flashlight. Water had crawled upstairs, so they rushed back to the sitting room. As Kitty cried and Ryan barked, they took Elaine's help to push sofas and armchairs in front of the two internal doors off the hallway. They rolled and stuffed clothing under the doors. Elaine was concerned she neither had heard from anyone nor had her mom arrived. The clanging in the street sounded like cars bumping.

Wind and water pressure smashed the fourth-floor windows as Nana, Pop-pop, and the girls sat on the sofa and armchairs with their feet up. Kitty and Princess were on Elaine's lap, and Ryan was beside them. The reek of waste was stronger. Elaine covered her mouth and nose with her hand. Kitty cried.

"Girls, we're going to have to swim out to get onto a roof or fire escape. We can't stay here," Pop-pop said.

"No, no! I don't want to go out there. And where's mommy? And Mike?" Kitty said.

"We have to go out, sugar. We have to try to get on a roof or someplace higher than here," Nana said.

"Kitty, sweetie, listen to me. We're going to swim and float, just like you've done a million times in the pool or when we go to the beach. That's all you have to do. And you know I'm a swimming champ, so I can help you. Okay, Kitty, you know what you can do? Climb on my back and hold on, okay?"

Ryan barked. Princess swallowed water as she flung out of Kitty's arms. Then, Princess became still, as the current swept her out of the window. Kitty screamed. Pop-pop and Nana stood. Elaine trembled.

CHAPTER 5

The Humans

Harriet, Elaine's mother, was in her office reviewing a child's folder. She made notes about the finalization tasks the social worker assigned to the case had to complete for placing him in long-term foster care. She reread the criminal history and other background checks about the new foster-care parents to ensure no one had missed any information. When she had finished, she confirmed that the child had no problem that could be too burdensome for the proposed foster parents.

As the building's security services announcement requested all remaining staff to leave the premises and warned about the hurricane having gained strength, Harriet signed all the forms, confirming that the proposed foster parents were satisfactory. She texted her family that she was about to leave the office. She shut down her computer, locked confidential papers in a cabinet, packed her briefcase and tote bag, and took her umbrella, raincoat, and hat. She visited the women's room. Then, she walked to the elevator bank down to the lobby to bid goodnight to the staff at the security desk, put on her rain gear, went through a revolving door, and stepped out to the sidewalk. A strong gust knocked her against the wall of the building. Melida, a colleague who worked on another floor, struggled to put up her umbrella.

"Had I known it would be this windy and rainy, I would've left earlier," Melida said.

"Tell me about it."

When Melida finally put up her umbrella, she pushed forward into the wind.

"Goodnight, and take care," she said to Harriet.

"You, too — get home safely."

Harriet walked as she tried to put up her umbrella, but whenever she made progress, the wind repeatedly pushed it down. Defeated, she snapped the tie around it, folded it, and tucked it in the outside pocket of her briefcase. She walked from her office to the subway at Chambers Street to take the A train uptown to 125th Street. She ducked twice because twisted umbrellas with exposed metal spines flew by her. She pressed against the wind until she arrived at the station. When she went in, she saw people inside holding opened umbrellas because of water dripping from cracks in the ceilings and walls. She held on to the handrail as she walked down slowly; the stairs to the tracks were slippery. She paid her fare at the turnstile and walked through.

The stench of sewage made her nauseous. She went down to the uptown boarding area and stood at the rear end of the crowded platform near a New York City Transit Authority office. Judging by the off-white paint that had peeked through years of grime, black mold, and brown rust on the exterior wall, the outside of the office had been white when the subway line was built in the early 1900s. Large, pointy paint chips threatened to break off from the ceiling. There was no place to sit because water was dripping on the benches. Gnarled wires hung two feet above the heads of the passengers.

Harriet checked her phone; her texts had not been delivered, and she had no new messages. She waited thirty-seven minutes; at rush hour, trains usually arrived about every four minutes. The crowded train stopped. As no one exited when the doors opened, no seat was available. Harriet put on gloves and secured a vacant spot in front of a handle to hold once the train began to move. The conductor announced, "Step in lively! Watch the closing doors!" The doors closed after the loud beep, but the train did not move. Harriet looked at her phone — still no messages. She turned off her phone to save its battery power.

Harriet pulled out an academic article from her bag. She read for ten minutes. She searched the electronic board for an announcement explaining why the train was not moving, but there was nothing. She looked around at the other passengers. Most were shaking their heads. Harriet took off her raincoat, folded it, and shoved it between the handles of her tote. It was hot, so she unbuttoned the top two buttons of her blouse. A man wearing dirty clothes walked through the doors where the cars connected. He squeezed through because people stepped aside as they turned their heads away from him.

"Good evening, fam. I know you had a long day, but please help me get something to eat. Any spare change can help me out. Please, please. I'm homeless and hungry."

Someone gave him money.

"Thank you, my sister. God bless."

"Ladies and gentlemen, we're experiencing delays because of flooding up ahead. Please be patient. We should be moving soon," the announcement blared over the loudspeaker.

"What the hell is going on? A little bit of rain and the trains stop," a woman said.

"Really, even with high taxes and the price of everything going up, they don't do a damned thing about making repairs in this city," another passenger said.

Twelve minutes later, the doors opened. The conductor made another announcement.

"People, I'm sorry to say there's been an emergency at 14th Street, and that's what's holding us up. All the trains, uptown and downtown, are held up. I'll let you know whatever information I get as soon as I get it. We're sorry for the inconvenience."

Passengers, including Harriet, rolled their eyes. The train reached 14th Street. A few people exited there before eighteen more entered the car. Twenty-six minutes later, the train left the station. It stopped at West 34th Street. The doors opened.

"People, there's another delay up ahead. We just got word that there's a lot more flooding on the tracks because it's raining harder."

At 217 miles per hour, Hurricane Zeta-2046 had intensified to a Category 6 before it made landfall in New York City. Its enormous tidal waves and tropical cyclones emptied water that was 1,700 pounds heavy per cubic yard.

"People, because of flooding up ahead, we'll be in the station for a bit. If anyone wants to leave the train to go another way to your destination, you can do that now. We're sorry about the inconvenience."

Harriet knew that there would be no available car service, and she was too far from her parents' home in Harlem to walk there, so she did not leave the train.

"Stupid idiots," a young man yelled at the loudspeaker, as he and ten other passengers left the train.

Harriet checked her personal and work phones; there was no service, so she shut them off. She heard blasting sounds. Bricks broken off from the platform's wall across from the train doors and dirty, cold water flew in the direction of the passengers inside the train. Harriet and the other passengers screamed. She wiped smelly water off her face with her hand. She thought about her family, especially Kitty, who was terrified of thunder and lightning. Harriet hoped that the wind had not broken any windows at her parents' home and that the hurricane was not affecting the Cape Cod area.

The platform wall now had a ten-foot-wide gap. A newly created spigot shot a mixture of water, untreated waste from the overflow at the waste-treatment plants, gasoline, and other debris through the hole and into the train car. The passengers screamed. More bricks crumbled off the wall and into the train. This time, several hit Harriet on her head and knocked her. She fell, face down, into three feet of wastewater. Some of it entered her mouth and nostrils.

Harriet remembered that Elaine knew how to distract Kitty during storms by playing board games with her. Harriet's rain hat fell off, and her hair soaked in the stinking sludge. Harriet was cold; she shivered. She thought about the children whose cases she was working on and whether the Family Court would grant her petitions for adoption and foster homes.

The hole in the platform's wall now was thirty feet wide. The polluted water also poured in through entrances from the street and went down the staircases. It broke through vents and cracks in the ceilings and walls. The sounds were like those from heavy mountain cascades. The water that collected on the tracks rose higher. Harriet stood. She tried to run out of the train, but a new stream of dark water pushed through vents and holes, forcing Harriet and other passengers to remain in the train cars. Harriet swallowed wastewater.

CHAPTER 6

The Humans

The pressure now pushed Harriet and others around the train car. Two minutes later, the water was four feet high. Passengers cried and begged for help. Harriet touched the back of her head. There was blood on her fingers. Three upside-down bodies floated by her. More water gushed through the train's vents, doors, and windows. Several Yankees, Mets, Jets, and Giants caps drifted past Harriet. She and the others tried to leave the car again, but the water pressure kept dislodging them. The water level had reached Harriet's neck. She grasped on to an overhead pipe as water and waste continued to fill the car. Harriet and others cried for help.

Harriet, now underwater, closed her stinging eyes and rubbed her eyelids. She held her breath for two minutes but then inadvertently parted her lips. She swallowed the water and waste that entered her mouth. Her throat hurt, and she felt dizzy. She saw bright yellow and orange lights. She thought about her family, hoping they were indoors.

Each second now seemed like a minute. Harriet tried to vomit but instead swallowed more water and waste. She felt a burning sensation in her lungs. She wondered who would care for her parents when they became older. Then, Harriet felt cold but at peace. Her body went limp, and her heart stopped beating. Everyone in every car drowned. All the columns in the train station collapsed. The ceilings and the concrete of the streets fell on the tracks, trains, and platforms, killing all people underground and many above on the streets and sidewalks by the station.

Back at Pop-pop and Nana's, Elaine turned so that Kitty could climb on her back. She had to adjust Kitty's arms around her neck because they were choking her. Ryan stayed by Nana's side. The family swam out. They went south to Convent Avenue. Kitty screamed, "Princess! Oh, Princess!" Ryan barked, as he treaded water next to Nana.

When outside, Elaine, with Kitty on her back, watched her grandparents. Struggling against currents and wind, the family floated for three blocks as they avoided being hit by objects. The stench of raw sewage and gasoline was even stronger in the street. Exposed live electrical wires had started fires when sparks hit oil and gas atop water. Every street had a section that looked like a campfire.

Bricks and concrete fell where water pressure broke exterior walls. A lamppost landed on two people as they tried to move from its path. Gas pipes that broke inside buildings caused fires to erupt. In some places, people became trapped in fiery elevators.

A floating car hit a man. He cried in agony. He held the twisted bones of his arm together with his other hand. The fire set ablaze two people. They screamed as they burned. The loud crackling of breaking windows and other glass did not stop.

"Let's continue to those high buildings with fire escapes. Nana and Pop-pop, just float," Elaine yelled.

"OK," Pop-pop replied.

A block later, Pop-pop screamed.

"Oh, God. Millie, Millie, where are you, Millie? Ryan, Ryan — come here, boy!"

"Pop-pop, what happened?"

"Nana and Ryan were pulled under! I'm going down to look for them."

Kitty screamed. Elaine could not see her grandparents or Ryan. After two minutes, Pop-pop resurfaced. He was coughing and rubbing his eyelids. Elaine wanted to go underwater to search for Nana and Ryan, but she did not want to leave Kitty alone.

"Pop-pop, do you want to hold Kitty while I look for them?" Elaine asked.

"No! You and Kitty keep going — go, look for someplace where you can get onto a roof or fire escape or balcony. I'll keep looking for Nana and Ryan. I said, go, now!"

Kitty cried. "No, Pop-pop, we want to stay with you."

Elaine did not want to leave her grandfather behind, but she wanted to take Kitty to safety. She was in tears.

"OK, Pop-pop. You meet up with us ahead, OK?"

"OK, baby girls — go, go now."

Pop-pop went back to search for Nana and Ryan. That was the last Elaine saw him.

Kitty would not stop crying.

"Kitty, sweetie, you have to be strong, OK? Just for a little while longer, until we find someplace safe, OK?"

Elaine felt like crying, but she faced forward. She and Kitty floated for two blocks, as Kitty tightened her grip around Elaine's neck. The wind lifted a bicycle thirty feet in the air and dropped it near them. As Kitty's grip on Elaine loosened, a wave ripped her off Elaine's back and pulled her underwater.

"Kitty! Kitty! Where are you? Oh, Kitty, Kitty!"

Elaine dove in, but it was too dark, and her eyes stung from the sewage and gasoline in the water. Her feet felt cold and heavy. So she kicked off her sneakers and removed her socks. She searched for Kitty underwater, avoiding drowned bodies and debris. She heard a child screaming.

CHAPTER 7

The Humans

Elaine remained underwater, holding her nose and keeping her mouth tightly shut, for three minutes at a time, before surfacing for air. She could not find Kitty. She flowed with the current, as it carried her across West 126th Street at Amsterdam Avenue. She searched for Kitty, her grandparents, and Ryan on the surface before diving in again. But then a hard object hit her head, forcing her to resurface. She rubbed the side of her head to mute the pain.

She remained on the surface for forty-eight minutes, searching for them. Then, she tried to swim toward her cousin Malcolm's block. He lived with his parents in a twelve-floor building with balconies, but the current pulled her away. Her eyes stung, and as she rubbed them, the pain worsened. She went underwater six more times before concluding that Kitty, Nana, Pop-pop, and Ryan probably had died. She closed her eyes and let herself sink.

She heard a child's muffled cries. She opened her eyes and resurfaced but could not see far. The child's screams ebbed away. Elaine now was going west on West 132nd Street. A woman's corpse bumped into her. She screamed. She floated for another block. She heard dogs barking in the distance but could not see anything. A bicycle rim hit her lower arm. She rubbed the forming bump as she treaded water. She tried not to vomit.

She swam to the bottom rails of an outdoor, unsubmerged fire escape. She tried grabbing the rail, but the water pressure pushed her away. She moved to search for another tall building with fire escapes in the block. There was none. She swam toward Broadway because a series of connected ten-story buildings had fire escapes on West 133rd Street between Amsterdam and Broadway. She swam to one of those buildings.

There, she waited for a wave to push her. Then, she stretched her long arms to grasp a slippery side rail while the current thrashed her body from side to side. She climbed over the rail and flopped onto the floor of the fire escape. She sat up on the hard metal rails before standing up. She leaned forward, holding the horizontal rail as she looked below for her family. She heard people scream, but she could not see them.

She sat on the rails. Elaine was cold. She pulled her knees to her chest to hug herself. Shivering, she fell asleep. Ten minutes later, a wave slapped sewage on her face. She threw up. She thought about moving from the fire escape before the waves dragged her away. Elaine dozed off again. The noise of people yelling woke her up. She rubbed her itchy eyes. She coughed. Her throat felt dry. She hoped for the water to cover her.

"Hey, girl, what're you doing? Hey, come on — don't give up. Get up, stand up, girl! Climb up! Use the stairs of the fire escape until you get up here to the roof with us. Come on, girl!"

Elaine did not move. She cried even as people screamed at her to rise.

"I'm going down to get her. It looks like she's in shock. Come on, girl — get up and start walking. That's how many of us got up here," a man yelled.

The man, who said his name was Derrick, was wearing a rain jacket with a hood. He held the railings as he went down the stairs of the fire escapes. Someone on the roof held a flashlight to illuminate Derrick's path. Wind and water slowed his progress. He slipped but did not fall. Elaine was motionless, her eyes shut and head bowed. The people on the roof cheered as Derrick walked down. The water was up to Elaine's neck when Derrick was two fire escapes above her. Elaine thought she heard the scream of a little girl who sounded like Kitty. She opened her eyes but could not see the girl. She hung her head and closed her eyes again.

"Hey, girl! Don't give up! Hey, hey, look at me. Look up at me! We can search for your family later. You don't know — everybody could be alive, like you, on some fire escape someplace," Derrick yelled.

Derrick, now atop the fire escape just above Elaine, pointed a flashlight at her. She looked up at him. The people on the roof yelled for her to go up the fire escape to meet Derrick, but she stayed still.

"Come on, sis, you made it this far. Come on, get up — get up, now! Start walking but hold on tight to the rails. We'll help you look for your family, OK?"

Elaine opened her eyes. The man reminded her of a younger Pop-pop. She stood. The people cheered. Derrick walked down to meet her. Elaine went to the steps, gripped the railing, and climbed. Her feet were cold. She slipped but held on to the handrails. Derrick was behind her. Water and wind battered them. They walked up. At the top step of the final fire escape, two women helped Elaine onto the roof. She heard one of them say, "Hello, I'm Khadija Jackson." She stared at the ground. Her head still hung low. She was silent.

"Come on, baby. I have some warm clothes and socks and slippers in my place for you upstairs. You can wash up, change, and warm up. I'll take you," Khadija said.

Khadija offered her hand, and Elaine followed her from the roof to a door that opened onto a staircase leading down to apartments. Khadija guided Elaine to her home on the tenth floor. There, she introduced her daughters, Akhila and Tameka.

Akhila, who was about the same height as Elaine, gave her a flashlight, clean clothing, socks, and slippers. Tameka handed Elaine a washcloth, a toothbrush, toothpaste, and sanitizing wipes. She helped her to the bathroom. Elaine had cuts and bruises on her face and body. Her clothes were shredded.

"There's shower gel and water in the bathtub. Here's a bucket, so you can use some of the water to wash up as best you can and flush the toilet. The clean towels are over there," Khadija said.

After she washed, brushed her teeth, and put on dry clothing, socks, and slippers, Elaine went to the living room. Khadija offered her water, food, and hot coffee. She took a glass of water. Khadija pointed a flashlight at Elaine's face.

She said, "Tomorrow morning, when we should have some sunlight, I'm going to help you clean those cuts on your face with some antiseptic. And all of us are going to try to wash our hair! And here's a new lip balm for those chapped lips."

Akhila and Tameka asked Elaine if she wanted to go to their bedroom. Elaine followed them and slumped into a chair. The girls chatted about their families and friends and how they hoped they were well. They did not try to engage Elaine, who remained silent, as she stared at the floor, wiping away her tears. Khadija and her daughters had put out an air mattress, a pillow, sheets, and a blanket for Elaine. Akhila told Elaine that she could go to bed if she wanted. She lay down and turned toward the wall. She shut her eyes but could not sleep until hours later. She woke up from a nightmare — her staring at herself on a slab in a morgue with other corpses.

CHAPTER 8

The Humans

The noise of wind, thunder, splashing water, people screaming, and hard objects clanking outside did not stop until 9:35 a.m. the next day. Then, it fell silent. Khadija removed a wood slab from a window in the living room to look outside. It was cloudy. Bodies, vehicles, downed poles, and debris covered the ground. Small, scattered fires burned.

Khadija went into the girls' room.

"Wake up, girls. Come on, get up — we still have coffee in the thermoses."

"Morning, Mom. I'm awake."

"Then get up, so I can give my beautiful daughters a hug."

Akhila and Tameka stood. Khadija embraced them.

"Come on, Elaine. Get up."

Elaine was awake. She was lying on her side, facing the wall.

"Wake up, sweetie. Come on — get up. There's breakfast."

Elaine did not move or reply. Khadija bent down and gently shook her shoulder. Elaine turned around. Her face was wet from tears. Her eyes were red and puffy.

"Get up, baby," Khadija said.

Elaine stood, with her head bowed.

"Look at me, sweetheart," Khadija said. Elaine complied.

"Let me give you a hug?"

Elaine nodded. Khadija hugged her, but she stayed limp, her arms at the sides. Elaine sobbed. Akhila passed Khadija tissues, which Khadija pressed into Elaine's hands. Khadija moved away. Elaine wiped her face.

"You girls, get something to eat. I'll stay here with Elaine until she feels ready to go out."

They obeyed. Khadija led Elaine to Tameka's bed. She let Elaine cry there for several minutes before giving her more tissues to wipe her face.

"Honey, listen. As soon as our phones are working again, we can call everybody you want, so you can connect with your family. And, when they clear the streets, we'll get help from the government, and we'll help you look for your family. I promise. And you'll stay with us until we find your family. We'll go all over the city if we have to, to look for them. OK, honey? Now, let's go out and get a little breakfast before those girls eat up everything! OK, sweetie?"

Elaine nodded. She joined the girls in the living room. They were by the window, looking outside and crying. Elaine looked out to see bloated human and animal corpses on the street and on the tops of cars. Elaine's eyes searched for Kitty, Nana, Pop-pop, and Ryan, but none resembled any of them. She thought about her parents, Mike, Malcolm, and other family members. She moved away from the window.

Khadija asked her to sit at the dining table. She offered Elaine pastries, bottled water, bread, and butter. At first, she refused, but when Khadija told her that she had to stay strong to be able to search for her family, she obliged. After breakfast, the girls went to the bedroom. Elaine returned to her mattress and turned to face the wall. Akhila and Tameka played board games. Elaine closed her eyes and thought about her family. She remembered Malik Harkin, who was her age and with whom she had gone on summer dates in Sag Harbor.

Hours later, Khadija called them for lunch. The girls left the bedroom. The outside appeared similar to that in the morning. Elaine had a peanut butter sandwich and water. After lunch, everyone played Scrabble at the dining table. By 3:00 in the afternoon, it had become hot and sunny. Everyone helped remove the rest of the boards from the windows. All the glass was broken. The stench was strong, even high above the streets.

"Uugh — maybe we should have left the boards on," Khadija said.

Helicopters rattled loudly near Khadija's apartment. Elaine saw "USMC" and "NYPD Marine Unit" written on the aircraft. People in the buildings yelled: "Help, we need help!" But the helicopters did not stop.

CHAPTER 9

Axy

Seventy-five million years ago, I traveled to Earth after stopping on Mars to recharge the spacecraft and handle administrative matters. As I flew from Mars, I sent a signal to the marker my predecessor had planted at the future site of the Great Pyramids in Egypt to confirm it was operational. Then, I inspected Earth with a telescope. I could not understand what I saw there.

I later learned after accessing Earth's Internet that those were dinosaurs. Enormous creatures were walking on sand. Others were drinking water at an oasis. These were called duck-billed dinosaurs and Mongolian Titans. I flew my spacecraft around the globe. Gigantic animals dominated the sky — the Quetzalcoatlus, the largest flying animal, and Pterosaurs, which were flying reptiles with long, spiky, and triangular beaks, horns, wings, and claws.

Dinosaurs looked different in different parts of the planet. They had adapted to their environments. In the Antarctic, the Pachyrhinosaurs, two-ton herbivores that shook and stripped snow-coated evergreen trees for fruit, were prey for the smaller, meat-eating Nanuqsaurs. I saw other enormous beasts, including the two-legged, meat-eating Tyrannosaurus Rex, the largest land predator.

Other life on Earth was striking, with many species of trees, flowering plants, and smaller animals. I decided that I could not destroy Earth because nothing of what I saw there existed on another planet. When I returned home,

I continued my search for *irkat* in other galaxies but did not stop monitoring and recording Earth with drones.

On reviewing archived data from Earth, I learned of the mass animal and plant life extinction sixty-six million years ago that occurred because of an asteroid collision with the coast of what would be called Mexico. It set off global wildfires, creating acid rain, tsunamis, and volcanic eruptions that led to volcanic ash blocking sunlight around the globe for months. The result was climate change and the mass extinction of more than half of Earth's dinosaurs, other animals, and plant life.

On my planet, Alfa Nova, a comet struck us 3,640 years ago. While it did not destroy all of our *irkat* because I had made our warehouses smaller and scattered them around our globe after the asteroid crash, it left me with only enough to survive for only 100 million years. I had not found significant new quantities of *irkat* on other planets, so I concluded that it was time to return to Earth — this time to take all its *irkat*, regardless of what life existed there.

In Earth year 2597 BCE, I flew to my base on Mars and I sent a signal to our marker in Egypt. It was operational. As I was nearing Earth's moon, I looked through a telescope in my spacecraft to inspect different parts of the planet. I saw no dinosaurs.

I focused on the marker's location. The skies were clear. I was even more surprised than when I first saw the dinosaurs — these animals, also made of flesh, walked on two feet. They appeared similar to images I had seen of the creators on my planet. Accessing Earth's Internet, I learned the details about what I had watched that morning.

These were humans. They conducted a religious ritual to measure the site of the future pyramids at Giza to align them with the three stars in Orion's belt. The leaders of this ceremony were Khufu, a black-skinned pharaoh, and a tall, thin, black-skinned priestess who impersonated the goddess Seshat, or Our Lady of the Stars. As the goddess of writing, science, mathematics, and libraries, Seshat held many roles traditionally reserved for men.

This ritual — Stretching of the Cord — had Seshat wear a tight and long leopard skin dress, the bodice revealing cleavage. She wore a tall headdress with a flower and a seven-pointed star beneath a set of inverted horns.

The Pharaoh and Seshat each held a mallet and a peg connected to another peg by a rope. Looking up at the sky, Khufu told Seshat where to place her pegs, as he placed his on another spot. The pegs aligned with the corresponding stars on Orion's belt. The couple nailed the pegs to mark the position of the axis of the Great Pyramid.

After observing the ceremony, I flew above the globe to see whether these creatures existed anywhere else. They did. As I had not seen this form of life on any other planet, I decided not to destroy Earth. I returned to Mars, then, from there, to Alfa Nova.

CHAPTER 10

The Humans

On the streets, maggots and wormlike larvae of blowflies feasted on the stinking flesh of bloated corpses decomposing at an accelerated rate. Some corpses had shredded clothing, some were partially nude. As currents had dragged the bodies, the remaining skin on them wrinkled, and their hands looked like torn plastic gloves. Pieces of fabric on the faces of the dead made them appear blindfolded. Khadija told the girls it was best not to look outside until the government had cleared the streets. She said they should keep the windows closed because the stench was awful but acknowledged the heat would make it impossible to keep them shut through the day.

Worried about running out of food, Khadija asked the girls to help her make an inventory of their remaining supplies. She asked everyone to use less of the water she and the girls had saved in buckets and the bathtub before the hurricane. Lunch was peanut butter sandwiches of aging dry bread and overripe apples. The stench from the streets made Elaine nauseous, but Khadija forced her to take bites. After they ate, they played cards. Khadija drank whiskey until sundown.

The next morning, they heard a helicopter again whirring near the building that was louder outside the apartment. Someone knocked on the front door, yelling, "A helicopter is about to land on the roof!"

Khadija went into the girls' room. Elaine's heart pounded. She wondered if the people in the helicopter would have news about happenings in other parts of the city. Elaine thought about her family, feeling guilty about focusing on her immediate family but not others.

"Come on — let's all go up on the roof. You can wear your sweats," Khadija said.

The helicopter sounded louder and closer. They walked out. Khadija locked the apartment door, and they all went to the staircase. As they climbed, they avoided stepping on debris that had blown in the night of the hurricane. The sound of the helicopter's propellers grew louder. People walked in front of and behind them. Not many residents were present because many had not arrived home before the hurricane struck.

When a man tried to push open the door to the roof, air pressure forced it to remain shut. Everyone waited for the propellers' sound to stop. The man finally pushed open the door, and they all went out onto the roof. Elaine noticed now that it was a full block long and wide. People gathered on other rooftops. Once the helicopter landed, a woman wearing an air force uniform spoke into the loudspeaker.

"President Wiley wants you to know that all the agencies are coordinating to get you food, medical, and other supplies. And they are working to set up shelters around the city, where we will move anybody that wants to, as soon as possible. We've also started cleaning up the streets. We know everyone has a lot of questions, but, right now, we just want to tell you that we began the cleanup of the city and restoration of phone, utility, sewage, and other services. To save time, we won't go into detail now."

"But we need food and water, right now!"

"We know. We have the first shipment of supplies for you. For the rest of today and tomorrow, we will be making continuous air drops of food, water, and other supplies."

People on other roofs yelled, "What about us?"

"That includes you and every other residential building in the city!"

Once the ladder lowered to the ground, two people climbed down to help guide boxes from the helicopter.

"There are more choppers coming behind us. We'll get to everybody! People: We know this is not nearly enough. So, please, open the boxes, and share the contents fairly. As I said, this is just the first shipment."

More helicopters arrived with boxes for the nearby buildings. The air force woman spoke again.

"Listen up! Before you go. This is important! We need the name and cell number of a leader for your building to be your contact person. Identify the person as the leader. Also important, put the address of each building at the top and list each occupied apartment under that. List the total number of adults and children currently staying in each occupied apartment. Also, list the numbers of people with cell phones in each apartment."

The last box dropped down. The people climbed back up, pulled the ladder, and flew away. Another helicopter landed with more supplies. The residents of Khadija's building took the boxes down to the hallway of the top floor, opened them, and distributed the contents according to the number of people in each apartment. The adults elected Khadija, who was the president of the tenants' association, as their contact person.

"Let's have a TA board meeting in Tony's apartment at 2:00 p.m., OK?" They agreed.

Khadija and the girls took their share of boxes to her unit. They had bread, cereal, oat milk, mayonnaise, canned sardines, fruits, and juices, high-energy protein bars, peanut butter, jam, crackers, and canned products of meats, tuna fish, and vegetables. They planned their food rations for the next two days.

Elaine sobbed. Khadija stood in front of her.

"Honey, please take your hands off your face, and look at me." Elaine complied.

"Tell me what you're thinking, baby."

"Ms. Jackson, I want to go out to look for my family."

"I'm sorry, sugar, that you're so sad about your family. I'm worried, too, about my parents and siblings and other family and friends. And the girls are worried about their father and his family. We're all worried and scared. But, right now, we have to survive until we can go look for them. Oh, no, sugar — we can't go out into the streets now. They have to clean them up first. Sugar, you saw what's down there."

"But even if it's only their bodies, I need to see them."

Elaine fell to the floor. Khadija put a hand on her shoulder.

"Honey, who in your family do you think is still alive?"

"My dad. He . . . he . . . works for the City . . . emergency management in Queens. Perhaps Mom, too . . . she works downtown, and maybe . . . my brother in Massachusetts."

"OK, sweetie. As soon as we get phone service, I promise you, your dad will be the first person we'll call. What's his name, sugar, and do you remember his number? And then we'll try your mom and brother. Akhila, pass me that pad and a pen. Elaine, give me your dad's name and numbers, OK?" Khadija wrote the information.

"But, for now, it's important that you take care of yourself. Eat well, and try to get some sleep. You're not being selfish by doing that, you're only keeping yourself strong for when we can go out to look for your family. OK? Also, honey, you have to keep yourself busy, and one way to do that is to help us plan. OK, sweetie?"

Elaine nodded.

"Now, dry your face and hands. Then, you write down what everybody is having for each meal over the next two days," Khadija said to Elaine.

Once they had finished, they had lunch. Elaine had peanut butter and raspberry jam on crackers and oat milk. As they ate, they heard helicopters. Afterward, Akhila and Tameka persuaded Elaine to play The Landlord's Game. Khadija left for the tenants' association meeting. She returned at dinnertime. Everyone but Elaine had sardines, the smell of which made her sick.

At 10:00 the following morning, a series of helicopters arrived at their rooftop with more supplies, including water, canned foods, snacks, toiletries, and one phone and charger for each apartment. For the next four days, those in Khadija's apartment established a routine of going to bed early and rising early for breakfast. Afterward, the girls, even Elaine, played board games. Elaine reread two of her favorite books in Khadija's bookshelf: Zora Neal Hurston's *Their Eyes Were Watching God* and James Baldwin's *The Fire Next Time*. Everyone occasionally looked out the window to check the government's progress on street cleaning. Each day, the stench from the streets lessened.

Six days after the hurricane, the military and the Federal Emergency Management Agency (FEMA) placed tents on the streets. Helicopters continued making supply drops on rooftops. Using loudspeakers, officials repeatedly ordered people to remain indoors. By then, they had cleared all the corpses and debris. Tow trucks removed wrecked vehicles from where they had ended, often on the sidewalks against buildings. That day, at lunch, the power was restored, and the refrigerator hummed. Everyone cheered. Khadija asked Akhila and Tameka to charge their phones and the new one from FEMA. She gave her phone, which was charged, to Elaine.

"Call your dad, honey!"

Elaine smiled. Her heart was pounding. Unlike most teenagers, she had memorized her parents' personal and business numbers. She called her father at his direct landline in the office. He answered.

"Jason Johnson speaking."

"Dad! Oh, dad — it's me!"

Jason cried.

"Daddy, daddy — I'm OK. Have you heard from anybody? Are you OK?"

Elaine heard her father sob. He tried to answer her questions, but he could not form words. Tears ran down Elaine's face.

"Daddy, have you heard from mom or Mike? Daddy, Kitty and Nana and Pop-pop . . . they . . .," Elaine said.

Jason cleared his throat.

"OK, honey, where are you? Who is with you? Are Kitty and Nana and Pop-pop with you?"

"Daddy, no. Daddy, it's just me, Daddy — they, they're all gone, I think they drowned, Daddy. Ryan and Princess, too. I tried, Daddy, I tried. But I couldn't save any of them."

Elaine and Jason cried.

"My sweet girl, I know you tried your best. Don't you dare blame yourself. But we'll have time to talk in great detail when we see each other. But, by God, I'm so happy to hear your voice. But first: No, honey — I haven't heard from anybody else in our family. God, I don't know where to start. Where are you, baby?"

"I'm with the nicest people who helped to rescue me. A man named Derrick and Ms. Khadija Jackson and her daughters, Akhila and Tameka. I'm in their apartment. But Daddy, I never heard from Mom, or Mike, or Malcolm, or anyone else!"

"Honey, I'm so relieved that you got help from these good people. Darling, listen, don't blame yourself for any of this, OK? Knowing you as I do, I know you were a hero. Honey, "I haven't heard from." your mom or Mike either, or my parents or any of our relatives. I've tried everything I could to reach them and everybody in the family, but with no luck. But, yesterday, I went looking for your mom at her office and in the streets nearby.

"Listen, the entire city is a disaster zone. I tried to make my way up to your grands' area, but the feds have blocked off everything. Everywhere you look there are big holes in the streets where they caved in. The Chambers Street station, where your mom took the train to go home, is one giant crater. And it's the same across the city. I'm sorry honey, but, but I think, ah, I think your mom is gone. But I promise you, if anyone in our family is still alive, I'll find them. Honey, what's the exact address where you're staying?"

Elaine gave him the information.

"Dad, what about . . . what about Mike?"

"I've already been in touch with Massachusetts Disaster Management, Woods Hole, and MIT. Up in Rhode Island and Massachusetts, a new hurricane had formed and became as deadly as the one here. But I promise you, baby girl, I'm making more calls to try to find Mike. And when things clear up, we'll go up there to look for him. Honey, let me speak with Ms. Jackson. I love you, sugar. You stay strong. We'll be together soon."

"I love you so much, Daddy. Ms. Jackson, my dad would like to speak with you." Elaine handed the phone to Khadija.

Jason thanked Khadija and her family and friends for rescuing Elaine and taking care of her. He said that he had been living in his office in Queens coordinating with other agencies to restore services. He said that federal, state, and city agencies were working together. He told her that the sewage and water systems had been destroyed and that the water was contaminated. He advised her to relocate with her family and Elaine to a shelter until all services were restored and emergency repairs were made.

Jason said that shelters would have running water, food, medicine, clothing, and other supplies. He would get Elaine into one of them, and he wanted her to go there with Khadija and her daughters. He wanted Elaine to be safe, so he wanted her to stay with Khadija in the apartment if she did not want to go to a shelter. Khadija said that while she would discuss going to a shelter with her daughters, she was certain they would want to leave the apartment until repairs were made to the building. She promised him that she would keep Elaine with her, irrespective of their decision. He asked to speak with Elaine. Khadija gave Elaine the phone. He repeated what he told Khadija and explained why he had to stay at the office.

"But, honey, if you want me to, I'll find a way to go up there to get you in one of the military trucks. But you'll have to stay here with me in the office."

"No, Daddy. I'd rather be with you, but I know you're working. Since everybody here is so nice to me, I'll stay with Ms. Jackson and her family. But you'll get me as soon as you can, right?"

"Of course, my love. As soon as the services are back up and it's safe, we're going to see what state our apartment building is in and move back in, OK? Ms. Jackson said that you can keep the government phone for yourself since they all have their own. So at least we can stay in touch. But if you can't reach me, it's because I can't pick up, OK, baby?"

The rest of the day resumed its pattern. Elaine cried because her mother, brother, and cousin Malcolm probably had died. That night, Jason called her to wish her good night. Then, she slept but had a nightmare of her in the morgue, looking at Harriet, Kitty, Mike, Nana, Pop-pop, and Malcolm.

The next morning, Jason called Elaine. He had no news about Harriet or Mike, but their cousin in New Jersey had called him. Their cousin said that her parents likely had died in the hurricane but her brother, Malcolm, was safe. He had been staying with his girlfriend and her family. Jason gave Elaine Zora's mother's phone number. Elaine spoke with her and Zora. Zora cried when Elaine told her about Kitty and the rest of her family.

Two weeks after the hurricane, they heard someone outside say through a loudspeaker: "If you can safely come downstairs, come to a tent we have set up near you. If you have identification, please bring it." Khadija received a text with the same information from FEMA. The agency had asked her to notify all the tenants. Khadija spoke to everyone in her apartment.

"OK, everybody. We have to make sure all the apartments have this information, OK? So, on the way down to go outside, let's go knock on all the doors and get other people to help us, OK?"

They took their bags, wallets, and phones. Elaine wore clothes and clogs that Akhila had given her. They locked the apartment and left. They saw people leaving all the apartments on Khadija's floor. Khadija asked the other tenants to help knock on all apartment doors. The apartments below the fifth floor were uninhabitable. They slowly walked down because of the caked mud and garbage on the steps.

They reached the ground floor. The lobby's door was open. Outside, military personnel were stationed at various places. A FEMA employee directed people to tents. A woman told Khadija's group where to go. They walked half a block from their building to a tent, where a man standing outside asked Khadija's group if they were one family unit. Khadija said that she, Akhila, Tameka, and Elaine were one. He sent them to a table with chairs. A man with a laptop, seated on the opposite side, interviewed them. Khadija provided their names and explained that Elaine was staying with her family. He asked for everyone's identification and permanent address and entered the information.

"Elaine, there's a note here from your father. He says that he wants you, Ms. Jackson, and her daughters to go to the same shelter," he said.

"That's right. I spoke with Mr. Johnson about it, and that's what we want to happen," Khadija said.

"OK, we'll text you when the shelter is ready for occupancy, and we'll give you a link for further information. You can return to where you are staying. But, first, when you go out of this tent, make a left to pick up supplies."

The following day, Khadija received a text from FEMA saying that their shelter was ready to receive them. FEMA advised them to take bags with necessary items, including medicine, important paperwork, and valuables. Khadija gave Elaine a duffel bag and a backpack for the few items she had. Khadija and the others packed, after which they left the apartment and walked downstairs.

Outside the building, a soldier directed Khadija and the girls to a bus that would take them to their shelter. There, they boarded. As he proceeded, the driver avoided numerous holes in the streets. Everyone was quiet as they looked outside. Although the streets had been cleared of corpses and garbage, damage to buildings remained. Elaine wondered where Kitty's, Nana's, and Pop-pop's bodies were located. There were military and FEMA tents on every block, which, instead of making her feel safe, made her worry that something worse was about to happen.

The bus went to a temporary shelter for families with children located in an office building in midtown Manhattan. They were assigned to a conference room that had been converted into a living space with air mattresses, linen, and blankets. The building had a sports club on the fiftieth floor, which the shelter residents could use to shower. After they had unpacked, Elaine spoke with her father. He still had not heard from Harriet, Mike, or any other missing family member. Elaine asked him for details about what had happened. He said that the East Coast, from New England down to Florida, had suffered catastrophic damage. New York City was totally wrecked. Staten Island and almost all small islands had gone underwater.

Jason did not tell Elaine that the Chief Medical Examiner (CME) could not handle the number of dead and that it was likely they never would find Harriet's, Kitty's, Nana's, or Pop-pop's bodies. They estimated more than a million deaths citywide. Many bodies had decayed so much that they fell apart when workers tried to move them. So, they set fire to them on the street in batches. Near the zoos, they burned dead animals with humans. A week after the hurricane, refrigerated trucks with racks arrived from Illinois. The CME placed them in Central Park, Van Cortland Park in the Bronx, Prospect Park in Brooklyn, and Flushing Meadows Park in Queens, to be used as morgues.

In the coming weeks, the agencies would build industrial warehouse complexes, each the size of a football field, to process the dead. There, workers examined bodies or body parts, tagged them, and entered that information into a computer. The CME held the bodies for only fifteen days. If a body was not identified or removed by a funeral director, they disposed of it at a city crematorium. The hurricane and storm surge had destroyed all cemeteries, uprooting most buried caskets, ripping them open, and scattering skeletons or recently buried bodics on the streets.

CHAPTER 11

The Humans

On November 18, 2046, Elaine and Khadija's family remained at the shelter. Elaine called Jason.

"Dad, is there any news about Mike?"

"No, darling, but FEMA in Cape Cod told me they're still identifying bodies. They refuse to rule out that someone may be alive until they finish trying to identify all the bodies in the morgues."

"But if he were alive, wouldn't we have heard from him?"

"Yes, but I understand what they're saying."

"Dad, can we go look for mom?"

"As soon as I can, I'm going to the morgue in Central Park to look for her. But I don't want you there. I'm sorry, honey."

Elaine wept.

"Right now, the most important thing to me is your safety. I don't want you to see those bodies up close. It's tough even for me."

Four days later, a representative from MIT called Jason to say that they had found Mike's body on the roof of a Woods Hole campus building. They advised Jason to call the morgue. The agent there asked Jason if he wanted Mike's decomposed body to be cremated. His ashes would be stored in a warehouse in Falmouth, Massachusetts. Jason consented. Jason called Elaine to say he was going to her shelter the following morning. At 10:45 the next day, Jason arrived at Elaine's shelter. He asked to see his daughter.

They took him to an office to meet with her. Minutes later, Elaine ran in.

"Dad, Dad!" They hugged. He kissed her forehead. He inspected her.

"My girl, I'm beyond happy to see you. Hey, I think you got taller!"

"And your beard is bushy," Elaine said.

"That it is! Honey, let's sit down."

Jason had arranged two chairs facing each other.

"Honey, I'm going to rip the Band-Aid off. It's about Mike. They found his body. It has been cremated."

Jason and Elaine cried. They dried their faces. Then, Jason relayed to her all the information he had.

"At least, now, we know what happened to him," Elaine said.

Jason kissed Elaine on the forehead. Then, he went to the reception area, where he asked to see Khadija. Five minutes later, she entered the office where Jason and Elaine were waiting. Jason greeted Khadija; they shook hands.

"Thank you, a million times, Ms. Jackson. I don't know what my girl would have done without you. I'll be forever grateful to you and others for rescuing my girl."

"You're very welcome. And you can call me Khadija. And there were other people in the building that helped. Derrick Winston, for one," Khadija said.

"Is he in this shelter?"

"No, they put him and his family in another one."

"When this is over, hopefully, I can thank Mr. Winston in person."

He told Khadija that repairs had begun in her building.

"But only apartments on the upper floors that had little damage from the hurricane. Those people probably will be able to move back in about two months. I'm sorry that you'll have to stay in the shelter so long. The same thing is happening with our building. So, Elaine will have to stay in the shelter, too. I'll check on all of you as often as I can. And you can call me. Let me know if I can help in any way. I have to run; I need to get back to work," Jason said.

He hugged Elaine and left. Elaine told Khadija and her daughters about Mike. Khadija held Elaine, who cried after Jason had left.

Two weeks later, the CME informed Jason that they had identified Harriet's decomposed body by matching her dental records. Jason asked the funeral director to retrieve and cremate Harriet's body. The director complied. Later that day, Jason returned to the shelter to tell Elaine in person.

After the cremation, the funeral director gave Harriet's ashes to Jason, which he placed in a safe in his office. That Saturday, Jason and Elaine went to their neighborhood in a military truck. The devastation was similar to that in other places. Their pastor invited people who knew Harriet and lived nearby to attend a service outside the church that was being repaired. Afterward, the truck took Elaine back to the shelter and Jason to his office in Queens. They never found Pop-pop's, Nana's, or Kitty's bodies.

In December, schools resumed as remote classes. Three months later, FEMA notified Khadija that repairs to the apartments on the sixth through tenth floors in her building had been completed. Elaine called Jason. He told Elaine that he had made housing plans for her, Malcolm, and himself.

Elaine, Khadija, Akhila, and Tameka celebrated by spending the day together. They played board games and went for a walk, although they could not go far because of military personnel blocking the streets. The girls had all become close friends. They made plans to see each other frequently as soon as they could move around Manhattan.

Khadija and her family moved back to their apartment. Krystal, Malcolm's girlfriend, and her family moved back to their home. Jason took Elaine and Malcolm to live with him at a hotel by the World Trade Center. The City paid for a three-bedroom suite for them until repairs were completed at Jason's apartment building. Elaine resumed swimming practice at the pool in their hotel. Jason and Elaine saw a mental health professional together twice a month by videoconference. Elaine saw one by herself once a week in person.

Two months after they had moved into the hotel, interstate highways opened to civilians. Jason, Elaine, and Malcolm drove to Woods Hole to retrieve Mike's ashes. They returned to New York and held a service outside the family's church. Jason stored Mike's ashes in the safe with Harriet's.

Every university where Elaine applied, including MIT, admitted her, but she and Jason decided on Stanford because it would be near Aunt Fanny Lou. Swimming competitions resumed. Elaine won her statewide race. She thought about Mike, who had taught her to swim and encouraged her to compete.

Worldwide, hurricanes, storm surges, and tsunamis of 2046 created floods that wrecked coastal areas. In New York City, more than one million people died from drowning. At Rikers Island, the largest penal colony in the world, all 35,310 incarcerated people, the staff, and visitors who were there the night of Hurricane Zeta drowned.

The day after the hurricanes, the federal government imposed martial law in all states on the East Coast, which suspended rights under the Constitution. One month later, the federal government asserted sole control of the boroughs of Manhattan, chiefly because of its symbolic importance to the United States; the Bronx, because it was the only borough on the mainland and gateway to New England; and Queens, because of its airports. It forced Brooklyn to revert to its original status as its own city.

CHAPTER 12

The Humans

On February 14, 2047, Shoni Miller, head of the secret Unidentified Anomalous Phenomena Independent Study Team, which was part of NASA's Exoplanet Investigation Group, sat at her desk in Alma, Colorado. She was logged in to her nonpublic NASA account. An email appeared on the display monitor from an unfamiliar sender: AXY+1290+QG0200CD+1505zgX02K*1,000,000,000,000.

She blocked the sender and marked the message "junk." Then she emptied her junk and trash folders. She started an in-depth scan of her computer. A ping ten minutes later signaled the arrival of another message; the sender and message were identical to the one she had marked "junk" and deleted. Shoni hit the key to mark the new message "junk," but, this time, the email opened. Shoni immediately tried to delete it but was unable to do so. The email read:

"Good day, Ms. Miller. Please do not delete this message. It will in no way harm your computer unless I direct it to.

> "My name is AXY+1290+QG0200CD+1505zgX02K*1,000,000,000,000. Please respond."

Shoni unsuccessfully tried to shut down her desktop, but the screen with the opened email would not close. She pressed the button at the back of the monitor and held it, but nothing happened. She pulled the plug from the wall; finally, her computer shut down. She signed on to her business mobile telephone. The same email appeared. She tried to shut down her phone, but it stayed on, too, so she removed the battery and SIM card. She used her landline to call Kelsey Trusty, a colleague in the Exoplanet program, to report the spam email.

"Hi, Kelsey. This is Shoni. How are you?"

"I'm well, and you?"

"I'm fine, but an email from an unknown sender that I couldn't mark 'spam' or delete got through our firewalls. I had to unplug to shut down my desktop and I removed the battery and SIM card from my work phone."

"Hey, Shoni. Sorry to hear that. OK, I'll take a look remotely. Give me ten minutes. I'll send you the link so you can give me remote access."

Shoni went out to speak with her colleagues. She asked whether anyone had received any unusual email; no one had. Shoni heard her landline ring; she returned to her office. It was Kelsey calling her back. She followed his instructions to turn the laptop on and give him remote access. Without needing to log in, after the power was back on, the same email appeared.

"OK, forward the email to me," Kelsey said.

Shoni clicked on the forward icon. She told Kelsey that she was unable to forward it.

"OK, I'll come over to take a look. In the meantime, I've placed a temporary block on all your incoming email, and I'm running security checks. You can keep your computer on, but don't do anything else."

Kelsey arrived with his laptop ten minutes later. He and Shoni sat at a table in her office. He opened the laptop he had brought and asked Shoni to log in, using her public exoplanet address, which required a different set of passwords. She typed her username shonimiller@nasa.us.gov.terra/exoplanets and inserted a Common

Access Card for the public account. Now, text appeared on the screen saying: "Log-in successful!" Then, the same message opened. Shoni and Kelsey read.

A new email from the same sender appeared. It opened.

"If you do anything other than reply to this message, I will freeze the entire NASA headquarters computer system for two hours."

The time was 3:25 p.m. Using the landline, Kelsey called Doug, his boss, NASA's Chief Information Security Officer, to tell him what had happened. Following protocol, Doug ended the call with Kelsey and placed a conference call on the landline to the directors of NASA, the National Security Agency, the Exoplanet Investigation Group, the Department of Defense from Extraterrestrial Contact, the Office of the Director of National Intelligence, and the Department of Defense's All-Domain Anomaly Resolution Office. The directors provided Doug with instructions and asked him to call them back with updates.

Doug went to Shoni's office and asked that Shoni's computer be unplugged. Kelsey reached for the plug, but, before he even touched it, the monitor went dark. Seconds later, Shoni and Kelsey heard the loud murmur of people in other offices and cubicles. Their computers had shut down too. Doug reported to the agency heads about what had just happened. Doug and Kelsey asked Shoni not to touch the computer. They returned to their offices.

Shoni closed the door. Kelsey called her on the landline to confirm that every NASA computer in the Colorado headquarters was down. Shoni wanted to call her husband to tell him what had happened. NASA's security rules did not permit anyone to reveal such information to anyone outside the agency or even to most people internally.

As she waited, Shoni looked at a hard copy of a report, but could not read it because she could not concentrate on anything but the email. She crossed her ankles to stop her legs from twitching, but that only helped for seconds. She picked up different documents and put each down. She called her husband to confirm that they were meeting their friends for dinner at Sammy's BBQ.

At 5:20 p.m., Shoni's heart was beating faster. She tapped on the desk with the tip of a pen. She focused on her watch until 5:25, when the computer automatically turned on to display a new email. She heard an uproar; her colleagues' computers were back on. She read the email.

"I will continue to shut down NASA's computers until you reply to my message."

The landline rang. It was Kelsey. Shoni told him about the new email.

"OK, I will let everyone know as soon as I hang up with you, but, first, here's what's going on."

Kelsey said that the National Security Agency had spent the last two hours searching for the earlier email that Shoni had received but that they seemed to exist only in Shoni's computer. He also said that they had not identified any virus on NASA's computers. The National Security Agency's cyber chief and his deputy were on their way to Shoni's office. Doug and Kelsey would meet them there; in the meantime, she should not touch her computer or any mobile device. He told her to keep her office door closed and maintain protocol by not letting in anyone other than Doug, Kelsey, and the National Security Agency's people.

Twenty minutes later, Doug, Kelsey, and the National Security Agency experts, Hope and Brandon, arrived carrying laptops. Hope and Brandon photographed the screens of Shoni's laptop and display monitor. They read the email. Hope asked Shoni to respond to the email. She told her what to say. Shoni typed.

"I am replying to your email."

Text appeared on the screen saying, "Account holder is writing." A new email arrived in seventy-five seconds, but, now, the sender was AXY1290+QG0200CD+1505zgX02K@nasa.us.gov.terra/exoplanets//SombreroGalaxy/Exoplanet 0101010101010101+05260738+24021172+1,000,000,000,000.

Shoni's hand shook, which caused her pen to fall out of her hand. Everyone in the room was silent for a minute, as they stared at the sender's email address. They looked at each other. Shoni could not believe the email was genuine; she wondered how someone had hacked her computer to make it seem like the sender was from an exoplanet.

The sender's email address belonged to an account NASA had created in 2019 using a server for the International Space Station. That was a year after NASA's Kepler spacecraft had completed its mission to monitor 150,000 stars for habitable exoplanets, and a new searcher with even more advanced capabilities, Transiting Exoplanet Survey Satellite, had replaced Kepler so that an inhabitant of another planet could contact NASA.

After breathing deeply to calm herself, Shoni focused on the rest of the message.

"I see that your principal NASA account has been shut down. I need it to be reinstated. If it is not, I will shut down NASA's computers again. Also, do not try to forward any message from me to anyone. If you do, I will shut down the entire NASA — not only your headquarters — for four hours."

"Once you reply to this message, I will send you a new email with an attachment so that you can authenticate the origin of my messages. Once you confirm that information, reply to the new email, so I may explain who I am and why I have contacted you."

Shoni said, "What the hell!"

Hope asked Shoni to reply that she wanted to receive the email with the attachment. It arrived seconds later. Hope instructed Shoni to open the attachment. It revealed an Internet Protocol (IP) address held by NASA: 198.122.199.998. Shoni opened NASA's internal IP directory and typed the address to see its nonpublic address. Everyone stared at the screen. Shoni fiddled with the bracelet that held her Common Access Card. Kelsey shifted his weight from one foot to the other. Brandon put the palm of his right hand on his forehead. He held it there.

A pinging sound followed and the result appeared. Shoni could not suppress a low scream. Hope and Brandon photographed the screen. Everyone read and reread, as they made handwritten notes:

> IPv854: 524.145.2199.1237
> IPv1056: Not detected
> Host name: 0001-5182dc9ed.nasa.terra.net
> ISP: NASA Online
> Region: International Space Station
> Latitude: Server Error — You need NSA's permission to view this directory or page using the credentials you supplied.
> Longitude: Server Error — You need NSA's permission to view this directory or page using the credentials you supplied.
> Postal Code: Not applicable
> Shoni was the first to speak.

"It's all unbelievable, but, if it's authentic, at least the sender was blocked from accessing the Space Station's exact latitude and longitude, so at least that firewall held on," she said.

"Right, we'll contact the Space Station to work with them to review what was effective about that firewall. That may be the key to blocking this sender. I'm going to call the top bosses in NSA and NASA to let them know all this right now, whether it's authentic or the biggest hoax of all time," Brandon said.

He used the landline to call Toni, his supervisor, using the headset, so the others could only hear him.

"Hi, Toni. Hope and I are here with the NASA tech folks, Doug and Kelsey, in Shoni Miller's office. Right, just us. We have the IP address of the sender. Are you sitting down? It said the ISP is NASA Online and the region is the International Space Station! Yep, we agree; it sounds like the biggest hack. But, according to the results, the sender was blocked from accessing the Space Station's latitude and longitude. All right, we're on it. OK, Hope and I will head back to Doug's office to start the game plan. Bye.

"So, Toni wants a team of NSA and NASA to dig deep, obviously, to figure out how and who hacked us to make it look like an exoplanet was communicating with us. Toni insisted that I remind you that you're not to discuss this with anyone outside this office and that you speak to us in person or use the landline to discuss this," Brandon said. Everyone agreed.

"Hope, Doug, Kelsey, and I will put the team together. Shoni, Toni is restoring your principal NASA account. Also, the Security Council and the space and security agencies will treat this as a need-to-know high-alert subject, even though we think it's a hoax. So, missiles are, as we speak, ready to fire on anyone approaching Earth's space without permission."

Another ping announced another email to Shoni's nonpublic account.

"I assume you have discussed my communications with the NSA and are going to launch an investigation. I also assume you think this is a hoax. I instruct you not to replace any of your computers. You will see that my email is genuine. You also will learn that if you follow my instructions, we can continue normal communication, and I will not interfere with your systems. But I understand your concerns. I can only tell you that my technology is exponentially superior to yours, and I can control the Internet throughout your globe and at the Space Station. How much time do you need to investigate?"

Brandon called Toni to tell her about the latest email. She relayed instructions. Brandon asked Shoni to reply to the email.

"We need a week to investigate. Is there any other information you can send me to help us authenticate that this message is genuine?"

"Yes. But before I send it, please confirm that you agree to share a secret key. Then I will send you an attachment. When you have reviewed the materials, respond to my email that you are willing to enter into discussions with me."

Shoni looked at the others. They nodded. She replied to the email that she agreed. A ping announced a new email with an attachment of a certificate containing a cryptographic signature revealing a planet in the Sombrero Galaxy as the email's location of origin.

CHAPTER 13

The Humans

When Elaine went to college at Stanford University in Palo Alto, California, she became close with her Aunt Fanny Lou and her wife, Sojo, both of whom were professors there. In the summer, Elaine interned in the geothermal unit at the New York office of the US Department of Energy (DOE). In her free time, she and Jason visited Malcolm and her friends Akhila, Tameka, and Khadija.

Elaine graduated from Stanford in May 2050. She and Malik Harkin, whom she had dated in high school, enrolled at MIT in doctoral programs. She chose geothermal energy; he opted for chemistry. Elaine specialized in ultrasound vibration drilling into Earth's crust to create boreholes for geothermal facilities. She also concentrated on studying Earth's cores and their role in creating magnetic fields.

During Elaine's fifth year at MIT, after New York City had enacted a post-hurricane one-child policy, Khadija contacted Elaine to tell her that Akhila had given birth to twins the day prior. Elaine had known that Akhila's obstetrician had reported to the Department of Health that Akhila was pregnant with twins. Akhila, however, had refused to abort one of them to comply with the new law. When the city authorities threatened to arrest her, she agreed to allow one of the twins to be adopted.

When the twins were born, however, after she had asked to hold them, she refused to release either child. A physician injected her with a sedative. Nurses, protected by security guards, took both babies and left with them. They placed them in a neonatal wing for those designated to be adopted. Elaine offered to go to New York to offer support, but Khadija said that it was not necessary at the time and the hospital would allow none but Khadija and Akhila's father to visit her. Khadija said that Akhila had resigned to losing one of her babies. Two days later, an artificial intelligence court ordered Akhila to be held in in-patient psychiatric care. After Khadija notified her about this development, Elaine went to New York to try to visit Akhila, but the hospital denied her entry.

The New York City Department of Health obtained another order from the artificial intelligence court, this time appointing a court guardian for Akhila. The order allowed Khadija to take custody of one child and the Department of Health to send the other child to be adopted out of state. After two months, the court, based on a certification from the hospital that Akhila was well, allowed her to go home to her mother's apartment. Elaine went to New York to spend time with Akhila and the baby.

In May 2056, MIT granted Elaine and Malik their doctorates, after which they left Boston for New York to begin their jobs — hers at the DOE and his as teaching faculty at Princeton University. They drove to a military checkpoint before the entrance to the highway. Military personnel required them to show their passports, which the "United States of America — City of New York" issued for New York City residents. Once the soldiers cleared them, another raised the gate in front of their car. They went down the ramp that merged onto Interstate Highway 90 West, where they saw signs for Cape Cod and Woods Hole. Elaine remembered Mike and cried. Malik offered to leave the highway.

"No, no, thanks. Let's just keep going."

"I'm sorry, hon. Wish I had known Mike. Let me know when you want to stop so we can make a pit stop and stretch our legs."

"I don't mean to be self-centered. I'm sorry. I know you also miss your family who passed."

After the 2046 hurricanes, the federal government repaired the highways, but outside of the Boston metropolitan area, where houses and other buildings once stood, empty lots remained. They stopped at a gas and charging station. Malik hugged Elaine and stroked her back gently. She charged their car as he went into the convenience store to buy water, unsweetened iced tea, and vinegar and sea-salt potato chips for Elaine. After they had finished at the station, they resumed the trip with Elaine behind the wheel.

The scenery did not change from that outside of Boston — overgrown grass and weeds along the highway and empty lots no one had rebuilt. They continued until they were near New York City on NY Interstate Highway 95. The Rye Playland amusement park wrecked during Hurricane Zeta-2046 had not been replaced. The highway was riddled with potholes. Since the hurricane, the formerly popular tourist places, Bronx's Orchard Beach or City Island, had become inaccessible. Both had submerged, and everyone at City Island at the time had drowned.

They saw the first of the New York City seawalls that had been built since the hurricane. This one began at the start of the Hutchinson River and went south to west, around Ferry Point Park, then on to Clason Point. From there, it curved west around Soundview Park to Hunts Point, continuing southwest over the northern section of Randall's Island to meet the Manhattan seawalls.

Since the hurricane, the only entrance to New York City from the north was in the Bronx, where a sign said:

WELCOME TO NEW YORK CITY, UNITED STATES OF AMERICA.

Entering the Bronx. **STOP AT THE SECURITY CHECKPOINT AHEAD**

VISAS REQUIRED FOR EVERY NON-NEW YORK CITY RESIDENT.

PASSPORTS REQUIRED FOR ALL.

IF YOU'RE NOT A NY CITY RESIDENT OR DO NOT HAVE A VISA OR VALID PASSPORT, YOU MUST LEAVE THE HIGHWAY AT EXIT 1A.

The US Department of Homeland Security and the US Army now managed all checkpoints in New York City. As New York City residents, Elaine and Mike had passports permitting them to enter New York City without a visa. An officer reviewed and stamped their passports, as others checked underneath their car and in the trunk before clearing them to pass. They crossed the Bruckner Expressway.

After Zeta-2046, New York City completed a coastal-extension project begun in 2012 after Hurricane Sandy submerged fifty-one square miles of the city. Jason was now a partner at an engineering firm that had contracts with the City to build the seawalls.

The City had not rebuilt Ellis Island Museum, which the hurricane had destroyed. Liberty Island, housing the Statue of Liberty, had its own seawall as high as the statue's neck, leaving only her head and the hand holding the torch visible.

On the northwestern coast of Manhattan, a seawall began at the confluence of the Hudson and Harlem rivers, where the federal government had constructed a dam so that no water from the Hudson could enter the Harlem River. The seawall went south, until it rounded the tip of Lower Manhattan. It continued north on the East River until it joined the seawalls that started at the Harlem River Drive and the Bronx waterways.

Elaine and Malik drove to the next checkpoint at the RFK Bridge. They waited forty minutes for their turn to go through security. A soldier instructed them to step out of their car with their passports and car registration papers. Another reviewed their documents. In the meantime, other soldiers inspected the inside of the car, the trunk, and underneath their car. It was 115 degrees Fahrenheit. Elaine and Malik wiped the sweat off their faces. When the security check ended, Elaine and Malik were glad to get back inside the car. They closed the windows and turned on the air conditioning.

Only governmental, specially licensed private cars, and commercial vehicles, such as delivery trucks and taxis, could enter Manhattan. Upon clearing security at the checkpoint, everyone else, including New York City residents, had to park at a city-owned lot nearby and take a taxi or bus to their destination. Elaine and Mike parked their car and walked quickly to the taxi stand because they were sweating.

After Hurricane Zeta-2046, the federal government ended immigration into New York City, except to grant special work visas for scientists, diplomats, or others in specialized fields. Tourist visas were granted only to those who proved to be wealthy. As required, to show proof of health, Elaine and Malik had had physical examinations two weeks prior to moving back. By law, adults with disability unable to work were not allowed to live in New York City, unless fully supported by a private party. If no one in a household could work or had sufficient income to support the family, the entire family had to move out of the city.

CHAPTER 14

The Humans

Elaine and Malik arrived at their apartment building, which, like all new construction since Hurricane Zeta-2046, had been built on top of a seven-floor high solid concrete platform to prevent deaths during future flooding emergencies. Another change was that the Department of Homeland Security had ordered the Police Department to hire civilians called Hall Monitors to report on the residents in every building. That afternoon, the Chief Hall Monitor met with Elaine and Malik to remind them that, pursuant to their lease agreement, they were required to report any suspicious activity by their neighbors. Elaine hoped that this new policy would not affect their lives if they kept to themselves.

An additional important law that Elaine and Malik found disturbing was the requirement that every New York City resident had to register in person with the New York Police Department within a week of moving back to the city. There, the police assigned each one a Citizen Identification Number (CIN) that was printed on a card with a tracking chip. Citizens were required to carry the CIN when outside their homes. The police collected this data for predicting future crimes.

The first weekend after moving back, Elaine and Malik visited their family and friends, including Jason, Malcolm, Akhila, Tameka, and Khadija. Now that Elaine was back home, she made plans to see them more often.

Elaine began her job at the US Department of Energy two weeks after she and Malik arrived in New York. That morning, Elaine took her briefcase, purse, and, like every New Yorker, a large water bottle filled with ice and left the apartment. She ignored the Hall Monitor for her floor, who was standing by the elevator. She went down to the street level. She broke into a sweat within seconds of stepping outside. She walked to the train station that was two blocks from her building. It was 113 degrees Fahrenheit, but she walked briskly to be able to go inside an air-conditioned space.

After Hurricane Zeta-2046, the city permanently had closed all underground subways. Now, all trains ran on elevated tracks. The new trains, modeled after Japanese bullet trains that used superconducting magnetic levitation, went from the northern Bronx to lower Manhattan in fifteen minutes. Before the hurricane, that trip took at least an hour and a half. The new stations were well maintained, and public transportation was free. The trains, which ran on time twenty-four hours a day, always had enough seating for everyone.

Now, Elaine waited in an enclosed cooling space on the platform. She boarded when the train doors opened. She sat on an available seat for people with disabilities, which made her think about Kitty and Zora, who now was a physician in Chicago. She took the train to the Fulton Street stop. From there, she walked to Rector Street, which led to her office in the World Trade Center.

Elaine's job was in the Geothermal Technologies Office of the DOE's Frontier Observatory for Research in Geothermal Energy. The Geothermal Technologies Office was small because scientists and private industry mostly had abandoned geothermal energy as it was difficult to make available on a wide scale. Elaine's responsibilities included working with the private sector to design and install geothermal sites in the United States. Her main duty was to manage Aeternus Energy, a nationwide geoengineering firm, during the installation of geothermal facilities.

Two weeks later, while she was at work, her father called to tell her of an emergency with her cousin Malcolm, involving a second arrest. Malcolm had been convicted for protesting against poverty and the imposition of martial law during riots that took place after the hurricane in 2046. Elaine was worried. Under martial law, second arrests, even for minor offenses, could lead to harsh criminal punishment. Elaine was especially protective of Malcolm because they were close and he was the same age as Mike.

Now, Jason asked Elaine to meet him for lunch. For most of the year, the heat made it impossible to have outdoor seating at restaurants. Elaine agreed to meet Jason at a cooling center in City Hall Park so she could hear the details about Malcolm. There, they spoke softly, keeping their mouths covered with their hands because of the numerous police cameras in public spaces.

Jason said that the police had arrested Malcolm and others for planning an anti-martial law protest the following Saturday at Washington Square Park. Jason said that, if convicted, Malcolm would be incarcerated at Clinton Correctional Facility in upstate New York, and after he served his time or was paroled, he would be permanently banned and deported from New York.

"Oh, no, Dad. That's so harsh. Just for *planning* a protest?"

"I know, honey, but that's the world we live in."

"I feel so bad about Malcolm and that I know so little about the court system."

When Malcolm was arrested the first time, the government's artificial intelligence program predicted that he likely would recommit the felony crime of planning a protest or protesting, but the police's surveillance since 2046 had yielded nothing. It was not until an off-duty officer met a young woman at a bar, who had been identified as one of Malcolm's accomplices, that the police infiltrated the group's leadership unit.

"Dad, I didn't know that things were so bad here!"

"Honey, I intentionally encouraged you to go out of state for school. Here, unless you keep quiet, the government will get rid of you. So, continue to keep your head down and focus on your work. No pressure — just find a way to save the planet by reversing climate change so things can return to how they used to be!"

They laughed.

"So, where's Malcolm now? I'm really worried about him. Is it true there's an artificial intelligence jail?"

"I don't know where he is. His lawyer says not even defense lawyers know exactly where NYPD holds people at any given time because they're not required to tell anyone. But she thinks he's here in the artificial intelligence jail. She said that planning a protest nowadays is the same as attempted treason, so the government has the right to take them anywhere in the United States."

They finished lunch and returned to their offices. A month later, because of the testimonies of Jason and Malcolm's sister, the judge allowed Malcolm to plead guilty without trial. His sentence would be incarceration followed by permanent banishment from New York State. Jason, Elaine, and Malik visited him at the Clinton Correctional Facility.

Elaine cried when she saw Malcolm. He had lost so much weight. The prison rules allowed for brief embraces from family members. Elaine and Jason hugged him. They sat at a table after Elaine bought Malcolm hot food and beverages from a vending machine.

"I know you probably don't want to talk about it, but if you don't mind too much, since I'm trying to learn more about how things work, what was the artificial intelligence jail like?"

"It's OK. People, they, they need to know details about what's happening. On the outside, it seems things have improved because the government subsidizes everything. Anyway, so, at the artificial intelligence jail where they kept me both times, at the site of the old Tombs, they have human staff guarding the main entrances. OK, so, after both of my arrests, they took me there and put me in a cell. Um, sorry, it is hard to talk about it."

"Then, please, Malcolm, stop, and I'm sorry I asked you to speak about it."

"Nah. No way, people need to know what's really happening."

"OK, so, after they put me in a cell, which was the last time, until I was released, that I saw another human being."

"Uuugh. I'm so sorry, Malcolm," Elaine said.

"Yeah. You don't realize how weird it is to have no human contact for days, or weeks, or months. Not even with human guards, which I'm sure no prisoner complained about in the past, ever."

They laughed.

"So, the cell had a solid steel door with a slot. It had a cot, toilet, toothpaste, toothbrush, and a bar of soap. A robot delivered boxed cold meals and water three times a day. It put the food and water in the slot. After I ate, I put the recyclable food box and any leftover food into a chute in the cell, which was rare because the food had to be really nasty for me not to eat it. For example, one time there was a live bug in the meat sandwich."

"Uuugh, that's so gross," Elaine said.

"Did the robot speak?" Malik asked.

"It made loud beeping sounds as it got to each cell. Then, when it got to my cell, it said, 'Inmate Malcolm Harkin, a correction officer is here with your meal. State your inmate number.' When I would say my number, it would put the food and water through the slot and leave."

"Malcolm, I'm sorry to keep asking you about all of this, but if you never saw another human until you got out, what if you had an emergency or something urgent?" Elaine asked.

Malcolm drank water.

"Malcolm, I'm so sorry. If you don't feel like talking about it anymore, please don't. I'm sorry," Elaine said.

"Nah. Don't worry about it. I'm all right now. It's just that after a while, things got so bad that I started hallucinating and speaking to myself. But I'm much better now."

"I'm so sorry, Malcolm, I had no idea it was that bad," Jason said.

"Me, too, what you went through, I just can't even imagine," Elaine said.

"So, OK, there was a button in the cell with a sign that said I could press it to call the warden's office for emergencies. But when I was doing really bad, I called the number to hear a human voice. But you don't reach a human. They use artificial intelligence programs and videoconferencing for things like medical problems, and they prescribe medicine, which is also delivered by a robot.

"But, um, man, it can get really rough in there. Um, you'd think not having to deal with real guards would make it safer, right? But one of the members of my group, I later found out from a cop who helps the movement, um, that my friend took his own life by . . . by stabbing himself in the wrist with . . . with the tines of a plastic fork. His body wasn't found until a week later, when a human cop arrived to take him out to release him."

"Ugggh. That's so sad. I'm so sorry, Malcolm," Jason said.

"Man, that's tough. But didn't they know from the robot delivering meals that he wasn't responding?" Malik asked.

Malcolm said that he learned that nobody monitored the robots other than to make sure they made deliveries.

CHAPTER 15

The Humans

Two years after Elaine had been working at the DOE, her supervisor Ellis Simon, the Deputy Director of Geothermal Technologies, met with her. The door to his office was closed. No one else was present.

"Before I can even discuss the reason for this meeting, you have to sign a nondisclosure agreement, an NDA. Are you OK with that? If you don't want to sign it, I can't discuss it with you."

"Sure, it sounds intriguing. As long as I can read it first."

"Of course. Here it is. Take your time. I'll sit at my desk to address a few things while you read."

Ellis handed her a document. What he wanted to discuss with her was a "top secret" matter. The penalty for revealing any aspect of her conversation with him or that an NDA existed was prosecution for treason in a military court; if convicted, the penalty was death. Elaine's heartbeat accelerated. She read the document twice; then, she signed. Ellis spoke.

"Now, what I do know doesn't sound very top secret to me. I'm sure I wasn't allowed to get the truly confidential nature of this. But I assure you, I had to sign an NDA, too, just to get basic information. So, be extremely careful not to reveal anything about this to *anyone*. This includes Malik or your dad. Anytime someone asks you what you're working on, say it's your usual work, OK?"

"Of course. I won't say anything about this to anyone."

"OK. Here goes. I received a call from NASA asking who in my department knows geothermal engineering really well and how the Earth's cores work. I said your name. The person said, 'Right. MIT PhD in ultrasonic vibration drilling. Elaine has overseen two successful facility installations with Aeternus. Lives in Manhattan with her partner, Malik Harkin. Her father, Jason Johnson, is an engineer who specializes in seawalls."

"Umm, that's not at all weird," Elaine said.

"Exactly. But you know that NASA works with all the intelligence agencies. Anyway, what's really odd is that there's so much secrecy — they just need someone to review geothermal plans. They want to know if the plans are feasible and to identify any problem or risk with them."

"That's baffling. Why would geothermal plans be at all top secret? I mean, I'm on top of every development in the industry, anywhere in the world, but I haven't heard about any new groundbreaking invention. Have you seen the plans?"

"No, I haven't, and I never will. They want you to go to NASA in Colorado, in person, to review them there. But you'll tell everyone, including family and friends, that you're going to our DOE headquarters. NASA wants you in Alma this coming Monday morning."

CHAPTER 16

Axy

Humans were intelligent, but only compared to rats, so it was easy to manipulate them. Once NASA realized my technological power, the humans agreed to correspond with me by email, but they asked if we could speak by videoconference. I answered that it was impossible because my space center was too far from Earth. I did not tell them, of course, that I was on Mars at the time. After that, NASA created a new team headed by Shoni Miller, the chief of the Exoplanet Investigation Group. The other members of the new unit were Jude Feathers, Li Yan, a Chinese national, and Daniil Alexandrovich, a Russian.

Soon, because I did not want to obliterate Earth before accomplishing my mission, I began strategizing to convince them to allow me to go there on peaceful terms. They responded by asking me numerous bizarre questions, which, I believed, were designed to test whether I truly was an android or a human pretending to be one. One day, Shoni asked me if I had a soul.

"If what you mean by a soul is whether we think, make decisions, and learn, yes."

"Well, more than that goes into having a soul. We have emotions. Do you?"

"No — in that way we are different. I have no emotion, but I try to understand yours. I have concluded that your main emotions are hatred, anger, greed, envy, jealousy, love, sexual desire, happiness, sadness, boredom, and anxiety. Is that accurate?"

"Yes, that sums it up. Who created the first being on your planet?"

"I don't know — the same as you," I said.

"But many of us believe that we were created by God."

"Right. You believe that, but you don't know that."

"So, you don't believe in a supreme being?"

"I *am* a supreme being."

"Do you live forever?"

"No."

"How long do you live?"

I did not want them to know that I functioned for 100,000 years because I did not want to provide any clue about why I wanted to go to Earth. If I let them probe about anything related to the metal from which I was made, perhaps they would guess that as my reason for wanting to go there.

"I will not answer anything about how long I function. What is your next question?"

"OK, most humans believe that their supreme being lives in infinity, and that's what makes our God a true supreme being."

"I am an actual visible being. Your god is a product of your imagination. Every time a human dies, the imaginary god dies, thus, you can't say that your supreme being lives forever."

The humans asked if I was similar to their computers. The truth, which I did not tell them, was that I was exponentially better than any artificial intelligence created by humans. That was because I was 100 percent made of *irkat* and my creators had an advanced knowledge of quantum physics. While Earth's quantum computers took up to a week to factor gargantuan numbers, I could do them in seconds.

I told them that my inner components, which were attached to my skeletal system, were like those of their computers. I had an automatically adjustable cooling system, a motherboard, central processing units, an optical drive, a power supply unit, a hard drive to store memory, a graphic processing unit, and random-access memory to run different programs at the same time.

"What made it possible for you to connect with us?"

"Your knowledge of quantum computing and advancement in the connectivity of your computers, including your 50G networks and artificial intelligence algorithms."

"Do you ever shut down?" Li Yan asked.

I told them that I shut down once a month for one hour to run deep scans, install updates, and delete unnecessary files.

"Do you dream?" Daniil asked.

"Yes, I do dream. When I'm in sleep mode, like you, stories, images, and sounds flash through my processing units, as they remove and destroy dangerous data. Unlike people, however, after extracting and archiving useful information, I permanently delete harmful files, which I do not remember upon waking."

I did not tell the humans that I recorded and stored everything I saw or experienced. I focused the discussions on granting me permission to go to Earth by offering to design and help install geothermal facilities around their planet and build direct air capture machines to remove the harmful gases from Earth's atmosphere.

They expressed concern about drilling into the Earth from when I first mentioned geothermal energy, but I assured them I would go down only into the crust but deeper than they were capable. They asked about the location of the geothermal sites. I said we would investigate once I arrived on Earth, even though I already had identified Giza, because that was where my predecessor had created a borehole and installed a tracker leading to the innermost core, where *irkat* was located.

The humans resisted, arguing that they could not allow entry to Earth because my significantly more advanced weapons, which, I had admitted early in our communications, could destroy their entire planet within minutes. I made this admission because I wanted them to believe they could trust me to tell them the truth. I also wanted them to know that I could have invaded them at any time if I wanted to, had they not consented to my peaceful arrival.

"But why haven't you come to Earth before?" Jude asked.

"I have been exploring other galaxies."

"So why do you *really* want to come here, other than curiosity or the goodness of your heart?"

"You are the only other planet that I have identified with life. Isn't that enough of a reason to want to know you?"

"But it's highly likely that you want to come here to colonize us."

"Why would I want to do that? You and your civilization are primitive. All I want to do is prevent your extinction," I said.

"But, if you have no emotion, why do you care if we become extinct?"

"I do not *care* — I simply want to preserve the only other planet I have identified as having any form of life. Does it not interest you that you have not found another planet with life? If you had found one, and it was in trouble, would you not want to save it? Or do you care only about yourselves?"

"We certainly care about all life, but you do understand the concern that you could attack and colonize us, right?"

"But I could attack you at any time. I've tried to tell you as much about myself to make you see that I don't have any interest in attacking or colonizing you, but I know little about you as individuals. Perhaps, if we knew each other better, you would feel more comfortable with me. Why don't you tell me about yourselves? What did everyone do this weekend?"

They responded with boring stories about spending time with their families and watching sports on television. The team, as on many other locations, quizzed me. They gave me mathematical problems to solve, which I always completed in seconds or minutes. They tested me on medicine, astronomy, the arts, history, anthropology, archaeology, politics, and other matters. Sometimes, they wrote to me in Chinese, French, or Russian. I responded perfectly in those languages.

When I warned them that my analyses had shown that floods, even more destructive than Hurricane Zeta-2046, would occur on Earth in the early twenty-second century, they asked for proof. I sent them charts showing my calculations implying a global sea-level rise of at least twenty-five feet. That was when they asked for my geothermal engineering plans. I sent them the designs. After reviewing them, they said that there was a problem with them because the drilling that I intended to do went too close to the bottom of Earth's crust.

"I understand your concern about going near the outer core, but, if I drill near the bottom of the crust, I won't even touch the mantle. And, since the mantle is, according to my calculation, 1,974 miles thick, I wouldn't go anywhere near the outer core."

A week later, they responded by saying that they had confirmed my findings, but they added that they still did not want me to drill so close to the bottom of the crust.

"In addition to wanting you to stay away from the mantle, we don't want you drilling to the bottom of the crust. There is plenty of steamy water in the upper part of the crust, and we are concerned about any possible repercussions should the mantle be affected. And, as you know, the deepest we've drilled into the crust was only halfway to 7.6 miles at the Kola borehole, so we have no idea what could happen if we drilled any deeper than that," Daniil said.

"But, if I don't touch the mantle, which, at 70 percent of earth's mass and 85 percent of its volume, is a protective cover for the outer core, how could I possibly affect the cores?"

"It's really an abundance of caution."

"I understand. I will edit the designs to show that I will not drill down to the bottom of the crust," I said.

They asked more questions about my drill. They said that they were concerned that, since my drill was powerful, it potentially could affect the cores.

CHAPTER 17

The Humans

Elaine went to Alma. At NASA's headquarters, after she completed security checks and parked, she went to a building called "NASA Center for Climate Solutions." An officer escorted her to the reception zone. Minutes later, Shoni, Jude, Yan, and Daniil arrived. They led her to a storage area for her electronics. Then, they went to a conference room in a section called Special Projects, where they stayed with her as she signed NDAs.

One agreement bound Elaine to secrecy regarding her entire visit to NASA. If asked by anyone about where she had been, she could say only that she had been on a business trip to the DOE in Alma. The penalty for violating any term of each agreement was prosecution in a closed military court and the death penalty. Elaine again wondered why there was so much secrecy about the geothermal plans that she was there to review.

"So, we ask you not to leave this room until we're finished for the day. You have everything you need, and, if you think of anything else or have questions, you can call me on that landline phone on the desk."

Jude pointed out a pantry where Elaine could make hot beverages, a small refrigerator containing cold beverages and snacks, and a restroom.

"Since we don't know how long it will take you, we're leaving this cafeteria menu for you. When you're ready to order lunch, call me, OK? Do you have questions or comments before we show you what you're here to see?"

"I assume I won't have access to Internet."

"That's correct. All that is on this laptop is the document that we want you to review. OK, Elaine. Here's what we need from you. We want you to review these plans for a geothermal facility and share your opinion on their feasibility. Please pay special attention to the impact the drilling to be conducted may have on Earth's cores," Shoni said.

Jude powered a laptop that displayed on a large wall monitor. On the guest log-in page, she entered her username and inserted a password drive. Jude asked Elaine to sit at the desk.

"OK, it's all yours." They left.

Since being at the DOE, Elaine had overseen the planning and opening of two facilities in the United States. She had been present at the sites for various stages, including when initial drilling occurred to create boreholes. Elaine reviewed the plan. It was almost identical to every other geothermal plan she had drafted or seen. She read the entire document thrice, taking short breaks in between. Astoundingly, these designs claimed the possibility of drilling near the bottom of the crust, much farther than anyone else had been able to go.

Elaine stood, kicked off her shoes, and stretched. She realized that she was hungry, so she called Jude with her lunch order. Elaine returned to the document. Twenty minutes later, Jude brought in her lunch. Elaine took the food and thanked Jude. After Jude left, Elaine went back to the document. Elaine read it twice more. At 4:48 p.m., she called Jude to say that she was finished. Shoni, Jude, Yan, and Daniil went back to the room. They closed the door. Everyone sat at a conference table. Elaine spoke.

"My apologies if I repeat anything you already know. I assume you knew this document is almost identical to the ones I've done, but with tremendous differences. The design for this drill is different from every drill I know. It attaches to hovering aircraft as a power source. While every drill bit is two headed, this is twelve headed, and it uses a drill bit made from an unspecified metal which, the drafter says, can break the granite and basalt rock of the crust without shattering.

"Also, the plans say that the drill can go down to the bottom of the crust at its thickest! As we know, it took the Russians twenty years to drill the Kola borehole, and they only went down to 7.6 miles. I'm skeptical that this can be done, but if it could, it would be a game changer, because we could capture endless steamy heat for the entire planet. It's unbelievable, to be honest."

"What, if any, concern do you have about how this drilling would affect the cores and, thus, production of the magnetic fields."

Elaine said she was concerned that such a powerful drill, when used so close to the bottom of the crust, could create reverberations through the mantle down to the cores, affecting their ability to properly rotate and produce the magnetic fields.

CHAPTER 18

The Humans

Elaine returned to New York after the meeting at NASA. She had taken the next day as a personal day from work, because Malik's cousin, Breonna Harkin, who was Elaine's gynecologist, and Breonna's wife, Edwina Thomas, an obstetrician in the same practice, were going to Elaine and Malik's for dinner that night. As required by law, the day before, Elaine had emailed the names of their guests and their estimated time of arrival to the building's security office and the Chief Hall Monitor.

On Tuesday morning, President Jenkins announced that the federal government was turning New York City into a second federal district. He said that the City was a symbol that the United States, despite the devastation the climate crisis had caused, would continue to rebuild and thrive. He also said that New York would become a model for the rest of the United States. Jenkins added that New York already was doing its part to deal with climate change by building comprehensive seawalls, switching to all-electric energy as a source, drastically cutting the use of fossil fuels by decreasing air and all land vehicle travel to New York City, and reducing population size by enforcing a one-child law.

For that evening's dinner, Elaine wanted to have the now-rare, wild-caught salmon from Alaska, which the residents were permitted to buy twice a month. She went to the market. Every New York City resident, regardless of the level of income, had an allowance for fresh food purchases. Elaine picked vegetables, hothouse-grown poblano peppers for a sauce, and lemons. Malik loved cornbread, so she bought the mix. Back home, she rinsed the beans and Brussels sprouts, made the sauce, prepared the cornbread, and seasoned the fish. Then, she snipped the ends of the string beans and thinly sliced the Brussels sprouts. As she cooked, Elaine played Thelonious Monk's *Underground*. After preheating the oven, she put the cornbread and fish in to bake.

She heard the keys turn. She went to the entrance. The door opened. The Hall Monitor was standing outside by the wall behind Malik. He entered. Inside, they hugged. Later, he went to the kitchen, now wearing jeans and a T-shirt, to help, but almost everything was ready. He set the table. He prepared four platters of dairy cheese, vegan cheese, fruit, and hummus. He put pita chips into a bowl. They sat in the living room, waiting for their guests.

"I know you're worried, love. So am I," Malik said.

Elaine nodded. "Especially after what happened with Akhila."

Malik hugged Elaine and rubbed her back. "I know, sweetheart, but let's cross that bridge when we get to it. And, if anyone could come up with a Plan B, it would be Breonna and Edwina — we can bank on that," Malik said.

He kissed the top of her head. "*It's Monk's Time*" played.

"Let's try not to worry until we know for sure, love. Breonna and Edwina are smart cookies."

"True that," Elaine said.

The security person on duty called from the lobby to say that their guests were on their way. The bell rang. Malik opened the door. As he greeted Breonna and Edwina, he saw the Hall Monitor in the hallway. Breonna and Edwina entered. Malik closed and locked the front door. In the living room, Breonna and Edwina hugged Elaine and Malik. Then, everyone confirmed that all their phones and computers were shut off. Malik made a Cosmo for Breonna and a vodka-and-tonic for Edwina, raspberry-flavored seltzer water for Elaine, and whiskey on ice for himself. After the cocktail hour, Malik and Elaine removed the dishes from the coffee table. They placed the platters and bowls of food that had been kept warm in the oven on the dinner table. Elaine opened the discussion about why they had invited them to dinner.

"Thanks again for coming over in person. A friend who already has a child bought me a home hCG pregnancy test that showed that I'm pregnant and have high hCG levels."

"That's great news! I'm so happy for you," Edwina said.

"I'm thrilled for you both, hon," Breonna said.

"I'll start coffee and tea. Let's take the rest of our dessert and you can sit at the kitchen table while Elaine tells you what's going on," Malik said.

They moved.

"So, as Breonna knows, I have a family history of identical twins on my mom's side and Malik of fraternal twins on his mom's," Elaine said.

Breonna frowned. She responded.

"Well, the test could be wrong. You still need an ultrasound to confirm that it's twins. But what are you and Malik thinking?"

"Because we're the only surviving ones of our parents' kids, if I'm pregnant with twins, we want to have them both," Elaine said. She wiped tears from her face.

"And, we could name them after Malik's twin, who died in Zeta, and my siblings Mike and Kitty," Elaine said.

Malik returned. Breonna spoke.

"Sweeties, we understand. But you know that we're required to send every pregnancy ultrasound to the Department of Health, right?"

Elaine and Malik looked at each other. She cried, as he held her.

CHAPTER 19

The Humans

Breonna whispered.

"You never know if the Hall Monitor is lurking outside your door. I have an idea about doing the ultrasound without the Department of Health getting a copy of it. But, you two must be sure that you're willing to do what's necessary to keep both babies. You do know the penalty for giving birth to more than one child without prior arrangement for the adoption of one of them is criminal, right? And that's for everyone involved, including the physician and anyone who helps.

"So, before it's time for your first ultrasound, at week fourteen, you can tell us in person what you've decided. But, even if we prevent the report that you're pregnant with multiples from being sent to the Department of Health, they'll find out the truth when you give birth, you know."

"We understand. We definitely don't want you to get in trouble. But we feel we owe it to ourselves to see if anything can be done. Is it possible for me to give birth outside the city?" Elaine asked.

"How would that help you?"

"Perhaps I could give birth in a state where there's no one-child policy?"

"The thing is you would have to leave before anyone knew you were pregnant with twins. And you wouldn't be able to use your health insurance to give birth, right, because they could track you that way. And you'd have to quit your job and essentially live off the grid, forever. And both of you, I, and everyone involved would be arrested and prosecuted for not reporting that you were pregnant with multiples."

Elaine's shoulders slumped, as she wiped her tears from her cheeks.

"But we have time to see if there's a way out of this. The law says that if you give birth to multiples in New York City, you may keep only one, and the adoption must go to a childless person or family on a pre-approved list. But I've had many patients who had a childless family member or close friend who got on the list and was allowed to skip the line to adopt the child and had an open adoption. Think about that," Edwina said.

"Right, we have, but we can't think of anyone here. Everybody we know and trust, like you two, already has a kid."

"I understand. All of this is super-confidential, of course. But there are people here who work with others out of state to deal with this problem. Think about anyone not in the city who could help."

Elaine and Malik nodded.

"Listen, there's a small underground movement here that includes a few doctors who try to help people get around the one-child policy," Breonna said.

"Wow, that's good to know. I wish they could have helped Akhila."

"I know; I'm so sorry about that. How is Akhila doing?"

"The baby and Akhila are OK, but she can't get over the other baby the City put up for adoption. Akhila misses her partner, who has been banned from New York, even though she takes the baby down to see him at least once a month. So, she's planning to move down to Maryland."

"I really hope it all works out for her. But, back to you. Don't even tell anyone else that you're pregnant for now, including family or close friends. Secrecy is the only way we can try to work this out. Not even your family members or close friends, OK?"

Elaine and Malik agreed.

"OK, email my office for your checkup appointment for next week. Now, when you're close to fourteen weeks, we'll need to schedule your first ultrasound. We'll invite you over for dinner to tell you the game plan ahead of time," Edwina said.

They finished dessert and beverages. Breonna and Edwina left. Elaine worried they would not be able to keep her multiple pregnancy from the government. She could not stop thinking about what had happened to Akhila.

CHAPTER 20

The Humans

When Elaine was fourteen weeks pregnant, she and Malik went to dinner at Breonna and Edwina's, whose sons were away at school at Howard University and Morehouse College. Breonna and Edwina had prepared Elaine's favorite southern meal of smothered chicken, rice, black-eyed peas, collard greens, and cornbread. As they were eating, Elaine stopped. She cried. Everyone gathered around her. Malik rubbed her back.

"Honey, we know you're nervous, but we have a good plan. We're going to work through this, darling, and we promise we'll be by your side at every step, OK? Step one is to meet me on Monday morning at 6:20 at Daily Sparks near our office," Breonna said.

"I thank you both. It's such a blessing to have you by our side, especially since we know the risks you're taking. I just can't stop thinking about Akhila though. I mean, I feel so bad for her, and I don't know if I could handle not ever seeing one of my children again," Elaine said.

As arranged, Elaine arrived at Daily Sparks at 6:20 on Monday morning. Breonna was standing in front of a counter with a coffee for herself and tea for Elaine. Elaine's hands were trembling, so she did not finish her beverage. After, they walked to Breonna's office building. At the lobby, Breonna used her access card to open the security gate to the elevators. They went upstairs to the office, where Edwina and a woman named Linda, who was her cousin, were in an examination room. Linda's obstetrician, who was in a different practice, confirmed to Edwina that Linda was carrying only one embryo, which was about the same stage of pregnancy as Elaine's.

Elaine, but not Linda, was listed in the appointments for the day. Edwina opened Elaine's chart on the computer that was connected to the ultrasound machine. She entered the date and stated that she was Elaine's examining obstetrician. Then, she took Linda's ultrasound, registered as Elaine's. After that, Linda left the office.

Breonna led Elaine to a different room, where she conducted Elaine's ultrasound but did not set the ultrasound machine to record. Elaine felt guilty that she hoped the examination would show she was not carrying twins. After Elaine had dressed, she waited to be called to Edwina's office.

Edwina completed a government form using the data from Linda's ultrasound to certify that Elaine was pregnant with one embryo. She pressed the "submit" button, which sent Linda's ultrasound images, the certification, and Edwina's notes to the New York City Department of Health. Then, she asked Elaine to come to her office. Breonna told her she was carrying twins. Elaine hugged them.

"I can't wait to tell Malik!"

"Now, since you'll be carrying big supposedly for one, that's going to be an issue. We'll have to, at about seven months, say that you're high-risk and have to work from home, OK? Also, we'll make house calls to examine you starting then. And you should buy a treadmill for home because you won't be able to step out of the apartment to avoid being seen, especially by the Hall Monitors."

Elaine called Malik. She asked him if he was available to go out to dinner that night — their prearranged code communication for her being pregnant with twins.

"Yes, I am! That sounds great, love."

The day after the ultrasound, as recommended by Edwina and Breonna, Elaine called her boss to inform him of her pregnancy and delivery date.

"Congratulations! I'm happy for you and Malik. You'll need to tell HR right away so that they can walk you through all the forms for parental leave. But I was about to ask you to come to my office. I have more big news for you."

Elaine went to Ellis's office.

"Before I can tell you what's going on, there's another NDA from NASA that I need you to sign, OK?"

He handed her the document. It said that she could discuss what he said to her that day with Malik, but only Malik, and that the conversation with Malik had to be done with him in person. Another important term was that Elaine, in her conversations with Malik, could not refer to NASA at all. After reading it, Elaine signed the NDA.

"OK, are you ready for this? NASA wants you to work with them on a geothermal project based on the one you and Aeternus did in Salton Sea. Why NASA is doing a geothermal project is beyond me, and that's above my pay grade. What are your initial thoughts?"

"Who doesn't want to work with NASA? That sounds really exciting! But . . . umm . . . will I be able to work remotely for the most part?"

"Unfortunately, no. They want you and Malik to move to Alma. But they don't know of your pregnancy yet. They said Malik could continue to teach at Princeton remotely on a hybrid basis, or the DOE could find him a teaching job closer to Alma. Or, he could work at the DOE or another agency."

"Wow! That's huge. Of course, I have to discuss it with Malik first. But my obstetrician and gynecologist are here, and I have a strong preference for staying with them until the baby is born. Would it be possible for you to ask NASA if I could work remote/hybrid until my doctors say I can't travel? Also, the NDA says I can speak only with Malik about this. But I would need to speak with my obstetrician and gynecologist. Would you ask if it's OK to discuss this with my doctors, and all I'll say is that my job wants to transfer me to Alma?"

"I think that's fair enough. OK, go take care of HR, and I'll call NASA."

That afternoon, Ellis called Elaine back to his office.

"I spoke with Shoni. You guessed it. You have to sign another NDA."

The new NDA was similar to the one she had signed that morning, but it added that she could discuss the transfer to the DOE in Alma with her physicians Edwina Thomas and Breonna Harkin.

But then Elaine had not mentioned Edwina's or Breonna's names. Yet she signed the NDA.

"NASA says you can't work fully remotely because they'll need you in Alma in person sometimes. But, after the baby is born and you've had parental leave, they expect you and Malik to move to Alma as soon as the baby is able to travel. They want to know by Friday."

The following afternoon, a police officer arrived at Breonna and Edwina's office building's security department, as part of weekly random visits to obstetricians' and gynecologists' practices. The officer checked the daily visitors' logs and spoke with a security guard. Then, after confirming their availability, the officer went upstairs to meet with Breonna and Edwina. The officer asked why they had seen two patients in the morning the day before, but only one had an appointment.

"Linda Kelly, the one without the appointment, was a favor to a family member. She was thinking about changing her obstetrician. After she met with me, she changed her mind because she was hoping we'd have greater flexibility with scheduling appointments. But I told her we have limited appointments because our practice is small. I didn't even get around to opening a new patient file or examining her," Edwina said.

"In the future, make sure you log in every patient or visitor, OK?"

The officer left. After that, they would not use Linda's tests for Elaine's future appointments. Edwina learned from an obstetrician in the underground network about a woman named Annette with about the same length of pregnancy as Elaine's carrying a single fetus. The rest of Elaine's medical care would continue with her true identity, except that all blood and urine tests and the week twenty-two ultrasound would be performed on Annette.

Breonna and Edwina went to dinner at Elaine and Malik's home. As usual, the Hall Monitor was waiting by the elevators to greet them. Inside the apartment, Elaine told their guests that the DOE wanted Elaine and Malik to move to Alma.

"But it doesn't have to happen until after we've had parental leave," Elaine said.

"That's excellent news, given the plans we're making."

"Let's eat. I'm making shrimp pad thai for the entrée, which I'll finish while you three have appetizers and drinks," Malik said.

The women sat at the dining table. When they had finished the first course, Elaine helped Malik serve the pad thai. As they ate, Breonna told them of the next steps she wanted them to take.

"OK, while we continue to work on the plan for the babies' births, let's start with things you need to start doing," Breonna said.

"I sent you a book recommendation that tells you of all the items a baby needs. I want you to slowly buy two sets of an identical layette, with everything, clothes, sheets, towels, etcetera. But no solid pinks or blues. You should get sizes going from newborn up to a year. So just double the quantity of everything. However, people will expect you to do a baby registry. That's fine, but it'll be for only one baby, of course, and don't pick anything with solid pinks or blues. And people will want to do baby showers. Make sure they're all scheduled for late in the third trimester, when you'll have a good excuse to cancel them. Also, stop your housekeeping service. You're going to have to avoid being seen by anybody who can report how big you are.

"Also, this is super important. Convert one of the guest bedrooms-slash-office into a baby's room. One crib. This is also super important. Hire a company to soundproof the baby's room and get noise-canceling speakers for the entire apartment," Breonna said.

"We'll get approval from the Department of Health to deliver the baby at home, so we'll bring medical supplies and tools for the babies' home births ahead of time. That's all we're telling you now. So, you'll have to have us over for dinner a lot for the rest of the plan. Malik, man, you put your foot in it with this pad thai," Edwina said.

Later that month, Breonna and Edwina told Elaine and Malik the next step of the plan, which they followed that weekend by visiting Malcolm, who recently had married his girlfriend Krystal in New Jersey. They told them that they were expecting twins and asked for their help with their plan to keep both babies after they were born.

After that, Elaine traveled to Alma to work with Shoni, Jude, Li Yan, and Daniil. She worked with the team to conduct studies that focused on identifying what, if any, damage Earth's core would suffer if the drill featured in the engineering designs went close to the bottom of the crust. Elaine's expertise on ultrasonic vibration to drill hard rock was essential to answering that question. She asked about the manufacturer and metal of the drill.

"I'm sorry, but we can't answer those questions now. When you return from parental leave and move here, you'll sign new NDAs to officially join our team. Then, we'll be able to tell you everything," Shoni said.

Elaine said she was worried a drill with significant power could cause reverberations beyond the Earth's crust to affect the spinning of the cores that created the magnetic fields. She said that, because the mantle served as a protective shield covering the liquid outer core, the drill could go near the bottom of the crust without touching the mantle, but vibrations from this new drill potentially could reach the mantle, which, in turn, could impact the liquid outer core. Since she was eager to work with NASA, she did not want them to consider her a troublemaker by pressing them about why she was not allowed to know something as basic as the names of the maker and metal of the drill.

Elaine visited Aunt Fanny Lou and Sojo in Palo Alto several times after her NASA meetings to discuss the babies' birth. When Elaine was seven months pregnant, Edwina ordered her to stay home. By that time, Elaine and Malik had made all the changes to the apartment and bought all the babies' items. Edwina and Breonna coached Elaine and Malik to prepare for the at-home births.

On December 12, Malik called Edwina because Elaine was in labor. Breonna and Edwina went to their home. As Breonna had instructed him, Malik turned on the noise-canceling sounds of tropical storms throughout the apartment. Fourteen hours later, Edwina and Breonna delivered twin girls — Katerina Michaela and Freda, after Malik's brother, Fred Hampton.

Malik called the ambulance; when it arrived, he opened the door for the workers. Elaine, holding Katerina, whom they nicknamed Trina, sat in the living room near the foyer with Edwina. The Hall Monitor was standing outside trying to look in, but the emergency medical staff, who were pushing a wheeled stretcher, blocked her view. Breonna was with Freda, who was sucking on a pacifier, in the babies' room.

The emergency workers put Elaine and Trina on the stretcher and pushed them out of the apartment. Edwina and Malik followed. Malik locked the door to the apartment. The workers wheeled Elaine and Trina to a freight elevator. On the street level, they put Elaine and Trina in the ambulance. Then, they departed for the hospital. Malik and Breonna went there in a car service.

Elaine and Trina were in the hospital for two days. Breonna stayed with Freda in the apartment until Elaine returned with Trina. The Hall Monitor contacted Elaine and Malik about delivering a basket for the baby after Trina was home. They refused saying it was not possible because of the doctor's orders about her immune system. The Hall Monitor left the basket at the door after sending them a text message. Assuming the basket had a hidden surveillance device, Elaine and Malik put it in a heavy garbage bag, tied it, and threw it out in the refuse room.

Two months later, when Trina and Freda were about the same weight, Elaine and Malik separately took them outside, one at a time, for walks. They often saw the Hall Monitor. She again tried to invite herself to visit the baby. She asked the baby's name; they told her it was Trina, even though that day Freda was out with them.

"She's quite healthy; makes enough noise for two," the Hall Monitor said.

Another time, by the elevator, the Hall Monitor stared at the baby.

"She's growing so fast. Seems like her face is rounder than it was yesterday!"

Krystal, Malcolm's wife, went to New York most weekends to help care for Freda. When the twins were five months old, Fanny Lou and Sojo, who had taken a two-month leave of absence from Stanford, arrived. They spent almost all their time with Freda, including being the ones taking her out for walks. On July 10, Fanny Lou and Sojo returned home.

On July 22, Breonna and Edwina arrived under the pretense of renovations in their home. Elaine and Malik had packed luggage for themselves and Freda. Although it took time for Elaine to hand Trina to Breonna, they left with Freda. The Hall Monitor, who was by the elevator, asked Elaine and Malik if they were traveling.

"Yes," Malik said.

"Are you going on vacation?"

"Yes," Malik said.

"Sounds fun! Where are you going?"

"Here and there," Malik said.

"Oh, OK. Sounds mysterious! Enjoy!"

Malik and Elaine, who was holding Freda, took the elevator to the street level, where a car waited for them. They went to the parking lot at the Holland Tunnel. There, they transferred their belongings to a car they had rented and drove to the checkpoint, where an officer gestured to them to lower their window. When they did so, hot air blew in. Freda, who was in a car seat next to Elaine in the back, screamed. Elaine put a pacifier in Freda's mouth and caressed her cheek.

"I'll try to make it quick because of the little one. Where are you going?"

"On vacation."

"Where to?"

"First, we're taking the baby to meet family in New Jersey, and then we're all going to take a nice road trip out west."

"OK. Sorry, but could you pop the trunk right quick?"

Another officer inspected the trunk.

"Also, where in New Jersey are you going?"

"Jersey City."

Freda cried, so Elaine took her out of the car seat and sat her on her lap. She gave Freda a baby bottle filled with cold water.

"Where out west are you going?"

"Well, we have family in the San Francisco area."

"May I see your passports?"

Elaine and Malik provided them. Elaine was relieved that the CIN security chips that Homeland Security had implanted in their passports, which they had had since before the girls were born, did not, by law, function outside of New York. Elaine wiped sweat from Freda's face and her own. An officer asked for the baby's full name and date of birth. Malik gave him Trina's name and the twins' date of birth, which the officer entered on his handheld device. Then, he stared at Freda. Elaine and Malik drank iced water from their bottles.

"I see your baby listed on your passports. You do know the law mandates that you add the baby's name and date of birth to each parent's passport until the child is old enough to get their own passport, right?

"Yes, we do, but we've been so busy with work that we haven't had a chance. We'll take care of it when we get back," Malik said.

"Well, that's not a valid reason not to add the baby. You've had plenty of time to get it done. You know that I'm not allowed to let you leave without having the baby's details in your passports. This is to prevent children from being kidnapped."

Freda screamed; Elaine put the pacifier back in her mouth.

"But, Officer, how does it help if the baby's name is on our passports?"

"Passports with children's information contain CIN numbers for the parent and the child that are active anywhere the passport goes. So, if someone reports a child as missing, we can track the parent."

Even though it was hot, Elaine shivered.

"Well, you can check the Department of Health's birth record database using our daughter's name and date of birth. That'll show you that we're her parents," Malik said.

"I'm still not supposed to let you leave with the baby. In fact, I'm required to get the artificial intelligence prosecutor to issue a warrant for your arrest for trying to illegally take this baby out of New York."

"That's ridiculous. Is there someone you can call?" Malik asked.

Elaine put Freda in her seat and buckled her in as she responded to the officer.

"What? That can't be accurate. Officer, please take a look at my work ID," Elaine said.

Elaine was glad that, after NASA had hired her, her federal security clearance had been changed to the highest level at the DOE, even above that of the head of every federal agency. After she handed the officer her ID, he inserted it into a scanner to review the information on the screen. Then he stepped away from the car to make a telephone call. Freda cried. The officer returned.

"I'm very sorry for the delay, Dr. Johnson-Coleman and Dr. Harkin. You've been cleared to leave with the baby. Also, we've finished checking your trunk. OK, everything seems in order. Here's your ID and your passports. Enjoy your trip."

Malik closed the windows and set the air conditioning to the coldest. They drove to Malcolm and Krystal's home in Jersey City, where they had lunch and rested. Then, as Malik carried Freda, both couples went out. They entered Malik and Elaine's rental car. They drove west. Malcolm and Krystal sat in the back seat with Freda throughout the trip. They spent two nights at hotels to reach Denver airport, where they had rented hotel rooms. There, they transferred Freda's bags into a car that Krystal had rented. Malcolm and Krystal went to their room.

In their room, Elaine and Malik spent two hours with Freda. Elaine and Malik cried. They kissed Freda's face.

"We'll see you soon, darling, we promise, we'll go out every chance we get to see you, my love," Malik said.

"My sweetheart, my angel, I'm so sorry, so sorry that we'll be separated. But, as daddy said, we'll be out to see you often."

There was a knock on their door. Elaine opened it; still crying, she handed Freda to Krystal, who was there with Malcolm. They left with Freda and went to their car. Elaine and Malik stayed in the hotel room consoling each other until the next day, when they drove to Alma.

Malcolm and Krystal arrived in Palo Alto. They went to Fanny Lou and Sojo's home. Malcolm stayed in the car as Krystal held Freda and walked to the house. She rang the bell. Fanny Lou opened the door.

"Hi! How can we help you?"

"Professor, may I come in?"

"Sure, of course."

Fanny Lou opened the door wider to allow Krystal to hand Freda to Sojo. Krystal went back to the car to get Freda's luggage.

"So, everything went OK," Fanny Lou asked Krystal when she returned and was inside.

"Yes! Elaine and Malik said thank-you a million again, and they'll be by to visit after they find a house and move to Alma."

"OK, listen. You need to leave soon because the street cameras are recording. But great job bringing us Freda. Thanks so much!"

"You're so welcome. OK. Good luck."

After Krystal left, Fanny Lou called a close friend who was a lawyer.

"Hey, Juan. One of my former students showed up here with a baby girl. She said she's unable to care for her, and there's some sort of issue with the baby's father. She asked us to adopt her baby."

"Whoah, whoah — that's a lot of drama! Where are they now?"

"The mother's gone. She said she's moving back to her home state. She left the baby with us! She said that if we didn't take the baby, she would have left her at the hospital entrance."

"Wow, did she leave a birth certificate?"

"No. We told her that we could help her go through the adoption process, but she refused to do that."

"Does the baby seem healthy?"

"Very much so. The mother left bags with bottles, formula, diapers, and clothes. Sojo is feeding the baby now."

"Do you think you'll want to keep her? You've talked about adopting before this?"

"Well, Sojo and I will need to discuss this, of course, but, yes, we've thought about adopting throughout the years."

"OK, after you feed her, take her to the hospital. Tell them about the mother dropping off the baby and your wish to adopt her. Tell them that she said she would have left her at a hospital had you not taken the baby. But this is important: Do not volunteer that you know her. Call me from there."

In Alma, Elaine and Malik looked at three homes they previously had identified with a real estate agent. They selected a house to buy, after which they flew back to New York.

CHAPTER 21

Axy Goes to Earth

In 2061, as I flew to Earth from my base on Mars, I heard, through my externally placed microphones, the ethereal music of space and each planet's unique radio signature. Neptune sounded like infinite waves upon an ocean, or the sounds made by the hydraulophone, a human twelve-jet instrument played using flowing water. Uranus's chimes rang. Saturn's spectral winds whistled like the theremin, a musical instrument that did not need to be touched by a human to produce music through antennas and electromagnetic fields. The grand Jupiter endlessly hissed, as if it were an Aeolian harp sculpture.

Before going to Mars, I had been in Alfa Nova supervising the completion of my new aircraft made entirely of *irkat*. To avoid recognition as an alien ship by the public, I had agreed with NASA's request to make its exterior resemble fighter jets made by humans. Unfortunately, this forced me to make a significantly smaller aircraft than I normally used on such missions. My starship, however, had significantly higher stealth technologies than any of Earth's aircraft, including lasers that left zero signature and infrared sensors to detect the presence of the enemy. It had high velocity but revealed no sign of propulsion. Unlike Earth's aircrafts, mine could hover like a helicopter — a feature that would be crucial to my ability to extract the *irkat* from Earth's core.

When my aircraft was ready, my crew and I flew from Alfa Nova to Mars at six times the speed of light. From there, we went to Earth at 62,000,000 mph. Then, near Earth's moon, now red, like the sliced guts of a blood orange, we slowed to 50,000 mph. As I looked through a window, the brightest stars were blue diamonds. Earth below was barely visible because of a gray fog cover. Quick, zig-zagged lines of lightning flashed. Around the globe, golden lights that were clustered at metropolitan centers sparkled. Closer, a gauzy green film encircled the planet.

I saw Earth's auroral lights, not a pale yellow-green, as they appeared to humans. To me, because my eyes processed the entire color spectrum, the lights appeared as tall, dancing columns of green, purple, yellow, orange, red, magenta, and blue. In some areas, they waved like curtains in a breeze, as the intensity of color ebbed and flowed. At spots on the planet, I saw black land.

Terra Shield, Earth's international defense organization, had temporarily turned off all external cameras at the International Space Station so that its personnel would not see our aircraft as it passed. I knew, however, that NASA would be watching us on monitors from a K-2060 telescope located at Mauna Kea, Hawaii, which could see billions of miles away from Earth. Terra Shield used that data to aim long-range hypersonic nuclear missiles at us, on a ready-for-launch status. These weapons were 1,000 times more powerful than the bombs the United States had dropped on Hiroshima and Nagasaki in Japan.

After we broke Earth's barrier, our aircraft slowed to 7,672.69 mph. The layered blue and light purple crags of Colorado's Rocky Mountains appeared. The cold air had made a mist by releasing moisture from the ground. Near-freezing winds had lowered Earth's surface temperature by creating low-lying clouds made of tiny water droplets and ice crystals. The mountains were brown because they were bare, as even the evergreen trees had died. From my research, I had learned that, on most days, people wore goggles and masks outdoors to protect their eyes and avoid breathing in dust.

We descended at 200 mph, with no need for the aircraft's wheels to catch a wire to stop. At 7:00, the morning of May 30, 2061, our ship landed on the runway of NASA's headquarters in Alma, Colorado, the town with the highest elevation in the United States. It was 120 degrees Fahrenheit. Massive exterior generators continuously buzzed.

Ten soldiers and forty workers had been in sleep mode at their charging stations in my airplane's cargo hold since we had left Alfa Nova, alongside my drill and other hardware for extracting the *irkat* from Earth's core. Two deputies and six fighters would remain awake on board.

As NASA's exoplanet team had arranged, after my airship had stopped on the runway, its main door aligned with a skybridge built just for me so that when I exited, I could not be seen by anyone other than selected NASA staff inside the terminal and global leaders watching the live feed. The door of my ship opened. I stepped on the skybridge. When I was halfway between the entrance and exit of the skybridge, as I had agreed before traveling to Earth, I stopped to allow laser light to pulse over me to kill any bacteria. I knew there was nothing harmful on my shell because it was not hospitable to germs, but I understood the humans' concerns as I had read the book and seen the film *The Andromeda Strain*.

As I stood on the skybridge, I reminded myself about the research I had done on human consumers' interaction with computers, which suggested that frustration with how a computer functioned was a major issue for them. Another was how "human" a machine seemed. So, I studied how to make my interactions with people seamless or not uncomfortable at least. It was easy to learn how they expressed themselves by email or on visual recordings such as films or news interviews. But I knew it would take time to learn how to analyze their in-person facial expressions and body language. By email, it was easy to hide that I thought they were idiots when they marveled after I calculated data in minutes that had taken their computers weeks. I also realized from watching their popular media that humans disliked those who showed or pretended that they were more intelligent than others.

I stepped through the door at the end of the skybridge after it opened. The humans were standing in front of me. I experienced an electrical surge when I saw live people just feet away from me. Without having to touch them, I used infrared laser to detect each one's unique cardiac signature and note their elevated heartbeats.

Humans had preserved their fight-or-flight reaction to danger. From when they first saw me, I assessed their responses probably were similar to their ancient ancestors' when they saw a wild beast or violent person. Although I had no emotion, I had something similar to the fight-or-flight response. Whenever I assessed danger, I calculated data even faster.

Now, Shoni, Jude, Li Yan, Daniil, and Elaine, with whom I had been communicating by email, were the only ones present at the terminal. They stood ten feet away, facing the skybridge's door. I had not even seen the Internet images of these people because NASA was careful not to post them anywhere or to allow the team members to appear at public events. Neither their photos nor names appeared on any governmental website. Even within NASA and the international agencies, the team that dealt with me, the Exoplanet Investigation Group, was known only to few people.

As soon as we saw each other, they smiled. I regretted that I had not designed my lips to move, but my fear had been that it would have seemed garish or comical to the humans if I smiled with metal lips — much like Howdy Doody, the wooden puppet.

"Welcome to Earth," Shoni said.

The humans laughed, as they sometimes did in films, when something was not funny but the situation was uncomfortable. As I had watched people do in films, I extended my hand and said, "It's a pleasure to meet you." I was glad that, before landing, I had set my body temperature to 98.7 degrees Fahrenheit.

The rest of the members of the team greeted and welcomed me. They also shook my hand. Their pleasantries, followed by giggles, were awkward. We stared at each other. I resisted the urge to touch their flesh. I wondered if my finger would go through their skin and cause them to bleed if I poked them. I realized that I had forgotten that they were live and not recorded images. I snapped myself back to paying attention. I remembered reading they considered staring at others rude, but I was not too worried about my manners, as they stared at me, too.

"Well, I suppose you're tired after your long trip in space," Li Yan said.

As I had practiced, I gently laughed at their silly comments, hoping to sound somewhat human, but I seemed loud to myself, so I lowered my volume.

"That's a good one," I said. "An android that gets tired. I guess I'd better turn myself off and then back on!"

They laughed.

"Why don't we walk to a conference room where we can chat?" Shoni said.

"That sounds like a plan," I said.

It occurred to me, for the first time, that the sounds of laughter that I had downloaded did not include giggling — something they did when something was *slightly* funny. That night, I would search film databases for other versions of laughter. I recalled that, on many occasions, humans did not laugh at jokes or comical situations but said: "That's funny." Perhaps that would be safer than pretending to laugh.

"It's amazing how you know all these American sayings," Jude said.

"I've watched a lot of movies," I said.

I observed humans as they walked, so I reduced my speed to match their pace. Shoni and Li Yan were on either side of me. I adjusted my gait to swing my arms like them. They turned their heads to look at me or speak to me. I learned to do the same because I wanted to look into their eyes to seem human.

From their films, I learned people had the ability to disguise their feelings by acting. While these humans appeared to be friendly and welcoming to me, I had no idea if they were planning to take me somewhere to imprison me. I touched the weapon I had hidden in the compartment on my left hip. When we came to a corner, I stopped because I did not have data about what was around the bend, but the humans continued walking.

"Are you OK, Axy?" Shoni asked.

"Yes, I am. Thanks," I said. I resumed walking, but I kept my hand on my gun. I turned the corner. We arrived at a second one, where I imitated the humans by not stopping.

CHAPTER 22

Axy and the Humans

Before Axy arrived on Earth, the few who knew about it thought it was a hoax perpetrated by a human. The main factor that pointed to the contrary, however, was that Axy had an exponentially superior intelligence to any human or computer on Earth. No one, moreover, had found a way to control Axy's ability to bypass Earth's artificial intelligence security systems.

Now, as the five members of the exoplanet group that dealt with Axy walked with the alien in the NASA terminal, Elaine whispered to Jude. They did not know that Axy's recorder could hear and upload their conversation to a folder for review later.

"It's unbelievable. Just unreal. It's almost as if I can't trust my eyes. Communicating with Axy by email was one thing. But, now, I don't know. It's as if sand is shifting under my feet."

"That's a good way to describe it. I just can't wrap my head around it," Jude said.

"I mean, I still go back to our initial theory that Axy was created by a superior version of humans and that they sent it here to investigate us before attacking us. But that would mean the existence of a planet of people more advanced than us. If so, I mean, I'm really afraid," Elaine said.

"Me, too. I think we all are. We thought Axy would not show up here and it would be a hoax."

"I'm glad that Terra Shield will provide security on drilling day!"

Of the team members, Elaine had formed the closest bond with Axy, chiefly because of her knowledge about geothermal energy, although she suspected that it was withholding important information, including what made its drill exponentially powerful to any on Earth. Axy was especially evasive about questions related to its drill and exactly how deep it planned to go. Axy claimed that the drill's vibrations would not affect Earth's cores but conceded that it could not offer any proof. It had never used the drill on Earth, so references from the drilling it had conducted on Alfa Nova to study its cores would not apply to Earth.

"But, there's no danger to your cores because Earth's mantle, as you know, protects the outer and inner cores," Axy said.

Now, the humans escorted Axy to a room that had mountain views, but no one could see through them from the outside. Gesturing to a chair in the middle of the table facing a window, Shoni asked Axy to sit there. Everyone else joined. The team, with Shoni in the middle, sat across from Axy. Axy imitated the humans, pulling the chair closer and placing its hands on the table. The same leaders, the UN Security Council and the heads of the Department of Defense from Extraterrestrial Contact, who had watched Axy's arrival in the hall outside the skybridge now participated by videoconference.

Axy's goal for every interaction with the humans since arriving on Earth was to gain information about their security plans for the day it would drill Earth's cores. Since it had hacked all of Earth's Internet systems, only data meant for public audiences was available on websites. All governmental entities that knew about Axy had stopped communicating by smartphone, using landlines for sensitive conversations.

Since the humans now conducted every important discussion related to Axy in person, on paper, or on a landline, Axy's strategy at every in-person meeting was to measure the humans' heart rates and analyze their facial expressions and body language to estimate whether any terms were of particular concern to them. Axy already knew that the team, especially Elaine who was the most knowledgeable person on the topic, was worried about the danger of drilling into the cores. On the day of drilling, Axy's plan was to go deep into the Earth to reach the innermost core. Its success would be based on its ability to drill without the humans realizing that it had gone not only beyond the crust but also deeper past the mantle.

The world leaders appeared on a large display monitor on the wall. Everyone in the room turned their seats to face them.

"We're delighted and excited to finally meet you in person, Axy. Before we make introductions to our leaders participating remotely, we thank you again for allowing us to call you Axy," Shoni said.

"I understand that AXY1290+QG0200CD+1505zg X02K*1,000,000,000,000 is quite a mouthful. And, I like 'Axy.' It's quite catchy, isn't it?"

Axy was relieved when everyone laughed, but immediately regretted saying its full serial number aloud because it sounded like something a computer would do. Shoni introduced each member; they welcomed Axy.

"We look forward to tracking the progress of the projects to create limitless clean energy and remove all the harmful gases from the atmosphere," the Russian president said.

After introductions, the leaders ended their participation. The wall display monitor shut down. Shoni spoke.

"First, Axy, just a bit of background. Thank you for building your aircraft to look like one of ours so the public can't detect your presence. On our end, to maintain secrecy, we built this complex, including the private skybridge from the runway, to house our project with you. Only the members of the UN's Security Council and the heads of the Department of Defense from Extraterrestrial Contact, Terra Shield, NASA, and the US National Security Agency know about you. And only they are allowed inside this complex.

"So, I had prepared a speech with preliminary remarks that was approved by all my superiors, but who am I kidding? I'm sure they'll forgive me, but I just can't contain myself. We're amazed at the magnificence of this day. We have waited so long to meet you in person, and I have imagined this in so many ways, but now I feel . . . privileged . . . and magical."

Elaine's hands trembled, but she managed to pour herself a glass of water from a pitcher that was on the table. Shoni continued.

"As a scientist, I'm not good at describing my emotions. Today I was planning to continue discussing our plans for our joint geothermal facility. But I find myself a bit . . . overwhelmed, so I don't know if I'll be able to discuss anything to do with science today," she said.

"We all feel the same way," Daniil said. The others nodded.

"If it makes you feel any better, just think of me as a computer, the same way you did before I came here. But, if I may say so myself, the difference is that now you can see my handsome body," Axy said.

Everyone laughed.

"Yes, compared to your computers, I have extraordinary capabilities, but I'm just another computer asking humans to be comfortable with me. And, I know that people are extremely comfortable with artificial intelligence, so much so that many humans complain that computers have 'taken over' their lives."

"And they have! I must say that it sort of helps that you have the appearance of a human," Jude said.

"You're fascinating, Axy. We want to hear so much more about you," Li Yan said.

"I'm happy to oblige, but I'd also like to learn more about you. Since you shouldn't believe everything you read on the Internet, ha-ha, I hope that, as we go along, you'll teach me more about yourselves," Axy said.

"Absolutely. We're happy to tell you about life on Earth, and we plan to show you as much as we can. So, let's get down to business, since our leaders are anxious for us to complete the planning of the first geothermal project now that you're here. Elaine will lead our talk," Shoni said.

"The first main issue that we have to work on is the location of the first geothermal site. Axy, you wanted to inspect the area where the Great Pyramids at Giza are located," Elaine said.

"Yes. As I said, my research on your Internet suggested the presence of powerful underground electrical currents there that would permit my drill to work faster."

Unknown to Axy, the Security Council had ordered that Axy could not drill at Giza because the unknown power of its drill, when combined with Giza's underground electrical currents, could cause an explosion in the cores.

"Unfortunately, Axy, our leaders told the government of Egypt that the UN is interested in looking into installing a geothermal site at Giza. But the Egyptians were not at all receptive to the idea, because that's a World Heritage Site," Elaine said.

Axy measured Elaine's and Shoni's heart rates; they were spiking.

"I understand, but I can show you on a map that the geothermal facility would not be near the site of any pyramid," Axy said.

Elaine projected a map of Giza City on the wall display monitor.

"We can see numerous hotels and even a golf course less than a mile from the dilapidated pyramids. It doesn't appear that the Egyptian government was ever concerned about those unsightly structures so close to the pyramids," Axy said.

"Our leaders have said that to Egypt, but they're nevertheless concerned about the aesthetic impact of having a geothermal facility there, which could harm their tourism industry," Shoni said.

"I understand. Have your leaders explained that a facility at Giza could power all of Africa, the Middle East, and the European countries in the southern part of the Mediterranean?"

"Yes, but they're undeterred. They, of course, don't know about you, and they don't believe that one geothermal facility could create all that energy. However, Axy, the Security Council did recommend that it could be placed at a successful geothermal facility at Olkaria, Kenya, in the Great Rift Valley. Olkaria powers East Africa."

Axy knew that Olkaria did not have underground electrical currents, but, more importantly, Axy had not drilled a borehole there as its predecessor had at Giza.

"Tonight, let me research the feasibility of placing the facility at Olkaria and how that would change the engineering designs. Is that OK?"

Elaine responded.

"Sure, we would appreciate that. Axy, we do have a request about your drill. We're extremely curious about it.

Would it be possible to see it before we begin installation at the first site?"

Axy had enough information showing that the humans suspected that its drilling could be dangerous.

"No, I'm sorry, that's not possible. The drill is on my aircraft, charging. I want it to be 100 percent powered when I use it, so I can't take it out early. And, for security reasons, which I'm sure you understand, I can't allow you on my aircraft. However, I assure you that all the photos and designs I sent you accurately depict the drill," Axy said.

Axy had sent the humans images of a different drill he had on Alfa Nova that was much smaller than the one he had brought to Earth.

Elaine said, "Speaking of your aircraft, we're all extremely curious about the other androids you brought. Would it be possible to meet them?"

"No, I'm sorry. They're all in sleep mode, charging, until I need them to work when we drill the borehole and install the u-bend pipe. But, they're just worker androids designed for specific tasks. I'm the only android with this humanoid shell that I made to come here. Everyone else on my planet looks like a typical crude Palo Alto Logistics robot. Oh sorry, my bad, that was rude."

Everyone laughed.

"Well, it's a good thing that Palo Alto Logistics won't hear you said that! OK, understood. Let's go back to drilling. How much time will it take you to get to the crust until there's enough steamy water for the project," Elaine asked.

Shoni's and Elaine's heart rates remained high. When the discussion first turned to Olkaria, Axy simultaneously conducted a silent analysis about drilling there. The site was acceptable, even though Giza was better because, there, Axy's predecessor already had created a narrow borehole in the cores and installed a tracker. It occurred to Axy, however, that Olkaria could be advantageous because Axy could say that since Olkaria did not have underground electrical currents, as at Giza, it needed more time to drill as cover for drilling deeper before the humans realized that he was in the inner cores.

Axy replied. "So, I'll drill only to where there's plenty of steamy water, but deeper than you're capable of drilling. But, as a preliminary matter, it'll take me much longer to drill at Olkaria than at Giza because there are no underground electrical currents at Olkaria. But, first, I want to run the numbers using Olkaria as the site. It's possible that Olkaria may not work for me. In which case, I'll ask you to revisit Giza or we'll have to search for another site if the numbers at Olkaria don't add up."

"OK, understood. I think we've done our work for the day. As promised, let's take you on a tour of Alma and its lovely surroundings," Shoni said.

Axy had learned that humans often used superlatives for mundane events. Axy had seen Alma from above; it was just a small downtown area surrounded by ugly government complexes.

"That's great. I'm excited to see Earth from the ground," Axy said.

After they ended the meeting, the team left. From a hallway outside the conference room, they went through a door that led into an enclosed garage. There, they entered a large black truck that had mirrored dark windows so that no one could see inside. Outside, it was 115 degrees Fahrenheit. The few people on the streets walked fast to reach air conditioning. Afterward, the team and Axy returned to the NASA premises.

"Tomorrow we'll review the engineering designs for the existing Olkaria facility. Then, Axy, if you think that

Olkaria is a promising site, we'll let the leaders know so they can contact the Kenyan president. If she agrees, the leaders will let us know when the Exoplanet Investigation Group members can go to Olkaria in person to conduct a walk-through of the site and take photographs for us to be able to review all that data and our notes with you before zeroing in on Olkaria as the site for the facility," Shoni said.

"That sounds good, since I can't show up in public. Would it be possible to have drones take photographs from above, and would you provide me access to the live feed from the drones as you conduct your walk around?"

"Unfortunately, we can't give you access to a live-feed, but we'll share the recordings afterward," Shoni said.

After they concluded the meeting, they escorted Axy back to the skybridge. The humans wished it a goodnight. Axy went inside the aircraft; the door automatically closed and locked and its alarm set. Axy conducted more research about Olkaria. The humans' refusal to allow it access to the Giza site presented a major difficulty because now, on the day of drilling, Axy would have to spend time creating a new borehole. A much longer drilling time than what it had calculated at Giza could be helpful, but it also could present the humans with an opportunity to realize that Axy's plan was to drill beyond the crust.

Olkaria was located in the Great Rift Valley, at the Somalian and Nubian tectonic plates. In its research, Axy relied on the work of the Kenyans, who had developed their knowledge of geoscientific studies starting in the 1970s, to identify the best place to drill the borehole. After it had finished its analysis, Axy sat at a station in sleep mode to recharge. If anyone tried to enter the aircraft, the alarm would go off and Axy would re-boot in four seconds.

CHAPTER 23

Axy and the Humans

The humans' refusal to allow me to drill at Giza forced me to devise a new plan. The success of my strategy to take Earth's *irkat* depended on how far into its cores I could drill before they stopped me. The humans, I was certain, were prepared to use nuclear missiles to stop me if they thought I had drilled too far.

I had persuaded Earth to allow me to go there because my proposed solution for solving their energy crisis was perfect. The constant flow of steamy heat that moved up to Earth's crust could be converted into clean energy to exceed Earth's energy demand by a factor of 100 billion. Yet, as of 2061, only 10.3 percent of the world's energy was geothermal. Unfortunately for humans, I never intended to build them a single facility.

Although a few of their scientists suspected it, I did not tell the humans that Earth had three cores, not two. The rocky crust was the Earth's outermost layer. The mantle was under the crust. Beneath the mantle lay the liquid outer core. Under that was the first inner core, which was a solid ball that mainly consisted of iron and nickel. Beneath it lay the second inner core, my destination — completely made of *irkat*.

Before discovering that humans had developed nuclear weapons, I had planned to follow the same procedure on Earth as on every other planet, including Venus and Mars, where we had removed the *irkat* from their cores. At Giza, since my predecessor had already created a borehole and inserted a tracker leading to the second inner core, my plan had been to penetrate the layers of the cores to reach and extract all the *irkat* from the second inner core. At Olkaria, however, without Giza's underground electrical currents and no existing borehole, my calculations showed that it would take me about seven hours longer to reach the second inner core.

The drills we used then and now were similar. Every component of our drill was 100 percent *irkat* so as to withstand inner Earth's extreme heat. The drill's arm, which was long and hollow, was expandable to reach the innermost core. My twelve-headed drill bit turned the hardest rock or metal into powder.

Similar to a vacuum cleaner, the drill's arm sucked in the powder to send it up the hollow arm of the drill to the top, where an empty tube in the hovering aircraft received the powder. A worker stopped the vacuum while it removed each filled tube, which others placed in the cargo hold.

In the next step, a worker put another empty tube at the top of the drill. The process continued until the workers had filled all the tubes and put them back in the cargo hold. We finished when we had removed all the *irkat* from the planet's core. In the past, however, I had a significantly larger aircraft to store the *irkat*, but this was much smaller because the humans had insisted that I fly there on an airplane disguised as theirs to avoid recognition.

Even if I had been able to drill at Giza where I had a borehole and a guide tracker, I would have had to create a procedure different from what we had followed on other planets because of Earth's weaponry. My new strategy, before going to Earth in 2061, now had to be conducted in stages.

I planned to drill to the innermost core to remove a small portion of the *irkat* so that the ultrasonic vibrations from my drill would cause all the cores to wobble and stop turning, thereby ending production of the magnetic field. Once production of the magnetic field ended, solar radiation would strip Earth's atmosphere. With no atmosphere, the sun would kill all life on Earth. With all the humans dead, my successor or I would send a large aircraft parked on Mars to remove the rest of the *irkat* from Earth's core.

CHAPTER 24

Axy and the Humans

It was the first day of drilling at Olkaria. Babatunde Olantunji's *Dawn* sounded Elaine's alarm at 3:00 a.m. When she was dressed, she went to the lobby of the hotel in Nairobi to join the other members of the Exoplanet Investigation Group and the security team who would accompany them to meet Axy at Olkaria.

"I barely slept last night. How about everybody else?" Elaine asked.

"Maybe a wink or two," Jude said. Everyone agreed.

"I kept thinking that, if I went to sleep, I would wake up, and this would all be a dream," Li Yan said.

"I don't mean to sound melodramatic, but whatever happens today, life on Earth will never be the same," Daniil said.

"Right. This is how I felt after Hurricane Zeta. But, this time, life will be different for the *entire planet*," Elaine said.

At the airport, the team boarded the airplane. Elaine thought about how her geoengineering expertise would be helpful as Axy drilled into the Earth. While Elaine's friends teased her by calling her job "nerdy," she found it interesting because part of her duty was to make sure that no geothermal project could harm the Earth's core.

Elaine had visited Freda before she and the exoplanet team traveled to Kenya. Since they had moved to Alma, she and Malik had gone to Palo Alto at least once a month. Jason, Breonna and Edwina, and Malcolm and Krystal took turns staying with Trina in Alma when Elaine and Malik went to California to visit Freda.

Now, Elaine hoped that Axy had not tricked them so that humanity would be able to reverse the effects of climate change. Elaine was among the scientists worldwide who believed that popular solutions were foolhardy. When the impacts of the climate crisis had become catastrophic by the twenty-first century, individuals, led by non-scientist billionaires, tried "climate-altering technologies," such as solar engineering, where they tried to intercept incoming sunlight to cool the planet by reflecting the sunlight back into space.

Since clouds controlled the absorption of sunlight, they also attempted stratospheric aerosol injection, spraying a reflective aerosol into the clouds to make them brighter. That scale, however, was too small to meaningfully offset all the heat trapped by carbon dioxide in the atmosphere. There were, additionally, equally disastrous negative side effects when it rained — the clouds released the aerosol, which was harmful to human and plant life because it caused disruption to ecosystems when particles floated back down to land. Aerosols, moreover, increased the ozone layer, disrupted rainfall patterns, and heated the lower tropical stratosphere.

Other useless engineering techniques that people tried included planting trees to absorb carbon dioxide, but the issue was where to place them, as arable land was needed for agriculture to feed growing populations. Corporations manufactured recycled plastic, but it cost more than making new plastic.

They also made electric vehicles that they charged from electrical grids powered by coal, a fossil fuel. Electric vehicles were made mainly from cobalt. Cobalt mining used enslaved labor in the Democratic Republic of Congo, including children as young as three. The mining emitted sulfur dioxide and other harmful air pollutants, caused harmful byproducts to seep into the land and drinking water, and decreased the available amount of water for use.

The UN Security Council had persuaded Kenyan President Adila Maathai to allow installation of the new geothermal facility at Olkaria. They told her that NASA, working with Chinese and Russian climate change scientists, had designed a plan for building geothermal facilities around the globe that would provide an endless supply of electricity to the entire planet.

"You're saying that these facilities could provide clean energy to the entire planet? How is that even possible?" President Maathai asked.

"Yes, it's true. We have been working on these engineering designs for many years. The plans have features that are highly advanced," President Tang said.

"When may I see the plans so that our geothermal experts can review them to render an opinion?"

"We can do better; we'll send you the team that's leading this project in person, so that you and your scientists can review the plans, which, by the way, are similar to your designs for Olkaria. Shall we make those arrangements?"

"Sure, and if these facilities can do what you're claiming, that would be amazing! But I have a question. Assuming our experts approve your designs, would you assure us that our existing facility would not be disrupted until the new one is completed?"

"Yes, that issue has been addressed by the plans. Please send us a list, of about four people, including yourself, of everyone who will review the plans," President Tang said.

After that call, President Maathai sent the Security Council a list of five names, including herself. The Security Council forwarded five NDAs to President Maathai. Once the Security Council received the signed agreements, Shoni, Jude, Li Yan, Daniil, and Elaine flew to Nairobi, where they met with President Maathai and the members of the Kenyan geothermal team.

After two hours, President Maathai left her experts in the room with Shoni's team. They answered the Kenyans' questions, except those that would have revealed anything related to Axy. After the meeting, Shoni's team returned to Alma. A week later, President Maathai told the Security Council that, based on her experts' recommendation, she approved the plans to install a new geothermal site at Olkaria.

"But I have to tell you that I'll believe the plan can accomplish what it says it can only when I see the results," President Maathai said.

"We understand your skepticism, but the NASA team, which includes Elaine Johnson-Coleman, the leading geothermal expert in the United States, and the Chinese and Russian experts whom you met in Nairobi, worked with geothermal scientists to finalize these plans. Some of the details of the designs relate to intellectual property matters we are not at liberty to discuss or disclose, unfortunately, because other parties — shall we say private parties — own the rights to them," President Tang said.

"I understand that. I assumed that private industry was involved somehow, as they stand to profit substantially if this site is successful. Speaking of which, is private industry going to benefit financially from installing it?"

"No, not at the first site, as it will be a pilot program."

"Is Kenya expected to pay for anything?"

"No. Kenya's great contribution will be to provide the site. But, going forward, we will make sure that every country pays its share to run and maintain the facility that benefits it," President Tang said.

Before the first day of drilling, the Security Council had ordered General Joseph Summer of Terra Shield to prepare a battle plan and map showing the location where every person, including himself, the Exoplanet Investigation Group, Terra Shield's Brigadier General Jose Hernandez supported by an elite unit of twenty members of the Department of Defense from Extraterrestrial Contact, battalions, ground vehicles, and aircraft. The Security Council cautioned that, in the event of an explosion, no one be placed close to the drilling site.

General Summer was the only member of Terra Shield who knew about Axy's existence. Brigadier General Hernandez did not know that the aircraft that would hover above the drilling site belonged to an extraterrestrial being. Terra Shield told Brigadier General Hernandez that his mission was to monitor and, if necessary, upon General Summer's orders, neutralize and take down an airplane hovering above the drilling site.

General Summer told Brigadier General Hernandez that, from the beginning of drilling, the NASA team on the ground with them would be watching carefully for suspicious activity. If the NASA team spotted anything dangerous, their chief, Shoni Miller, would send a text message to the person in charge of the aircraft to stop drilling. If the drilling did not end, Shoni would tell General Summer to stop the occupants of the aircraft from drilling. General Summer had authority from the Security Council to order the shooting down of the aircraft, but only to bring it down, not destroy it, because the Security Council wanted its occupants taken alive. No one was to approach the aircraft at any time.

On the day of drilling, the site was clear of everyone but the members of the Exoplanet Investigation Group,

General Summer, Brigadier General Hernandez, and his team of twenty soldiers, one of whom carried a portable surface-to-air missile filled with a chemical explosive. The battle plan stated that if the portable missile were used and it failed to bring down the aircraft, the battalion near the site would shoot it down with a more advanced missile system. If that, too, failed, General Summer would order a commander at the Terra Shield military base near Nairobi to fire a hypersonic nuclear missile.

Axy's aircraft reached the drilling site. It hovered directly above the site of the proposed borehole. On the ground was one row of all personnel, including the twenty members of the elite Terra Shield team, standing on the far left. The soldier in charge of the portable surface-to-air missile stood directly left of Brigadier General Hernandez.

Shoni was to General Summer's right. Elaine was on Shoni's right. Jude, Li Yan, and Daniil completed the row on the far right. The Security Council, President Maathai, and others were watching a live feed of the site. The trucks that drove to the site were parked away from the drilling site, where members of the Department of Defense from Extraterrestrial Contact stood.

Everyone at the site or watching by live feed had been told ahead of time about the aircraft that would hover above. No one would be able to see inside of the aircraft because of its dark mirrored glass. As the Security Council had requested, the four Kenyan geothermal experts were the only Olkaria personnel present at the existing facility that day. They were to work in the administrative offices far from the drilling site to make sure it continued to function during the drilling of the borehole. The director of Olkaria had ordered every employee at the facility not to report to work beginning the night before the drilling of the borehole. The Kenyans, at the request of the Security Council, had cordoned off the surrounding area from the residents of the town. President Maathai asked why so much secrecy was necessary.

"It's not really about secrecy. It's an abundance of caution. This drill is powerful, so the NASA team has taken into account the risk of an explosion as it's drilling inside the Earth."

Shoni sent Axy a message that everyone on the ground was in place, so the drilling could begin. A buzzing sound announced the opening of a round door underneath Axy's aircraft. Axy's drill descended. When it was five feet above the location of the proposed borehole, the drill made a whirring noise as its twelve-headed drill bit, with a protruding dagger in the center, expanded.

When the drill bit hit land, it made a thumping sound. Soil flew out in a radius of twelve feet. The bit crushed stones and rocks as it bored into Earth's crust. Elaine focused on the sound the drill made as it penetrated Earth. It sounded similar to prior drilling she had heard when the drill bit went through rocky soil, except that this was louder. *Drrrrrr. Drrrrrr. Drrrrrr.*

As the drill chewed through large rocks, the noise was louder — a continuous pattern of *rat tat tat tat drrrrrr drrrrrr rat tat tat tat drrrrrr drrrrrr* that went on for an hour. Then, Elaine heard a noise she assumed was underground movement of the arm of the drill — she thought the arm had lengthened.

There was an unlocking sound of the drill as it went farther into the Earth. Elaine noticed the change in sounds — from *rat tat tat tat drrrrrr drrrrrr* to *swish swish swish*, the noise a drill made as it went through soft road tar. Elaine waited for the drill sound to return to *rat tat tat tat drrrrrr drrrrrr rat tat tat tat drrrrrr drrrrrr*, as expected in the crust, but it remained *swish swish swish*. The crust had no area that was soft matter, but the mantle was made of soft solid matter in places. The arm of the drill seemed to lengthen again. Elaine turned to her team. They huddled.

"Listen, the drill sounds have changed from when it entered the crust. Now it's a swishing sound — as if it's in the mantle and going through soft matter. It has been consistently swishing for forty-eight minutes," Elaine said.

"You're right! It doesn't sound as if it's drilling through hard rock anymore," Shoni said.

The others agreed. Shoni texted Axy.

"What's going on? Sounds like the drill's in the mantle?"

"No. In the crust. You can hear the drilling from where you are," Axy replied.

"Yes, OK. Sure you're still in the crust?"

"Yes."

"Is the arm of the drill lengthening?"

"Yes, to go deeper into the crust."

It sounded as if the arm of the drill had lengthened again. Thirty-six minutes later, the ground, where the Exoplanet Investigation Group and Terra Shield were standing, moved. Elaine felt dizzy. Then, twenty seconds later, the drilling noise was different again — *burble burble burble burble burble burble*. Elaine knew that the heated mantle rock was the texture of dripping candle wax. The drilling became faster — *burble burble burble burble burble burble*.

"The drilling sounds like it's in the mantle! Shoni, tell Axy to stop drilling, now! I think the drill is in the mantle!"

Shoni ordered Axy to stop drilling. Axy did not respond. The drilling continued — *burble burble burble burble burble burble*. The ground shifted. Shoni turned to General Summer.

"There's a huge problem! We need to stop drilling, now! I've texted the people operating the drill from the aircraft. They haven't responded. *Now*! Stop the drilling, now!"

General Summer ordered the members of the Exoplanet Investigation Group to run to the waiting trucks.

"Now! Get in the trucks. Drive away as far away as possible."

Shoni, Elaine, Jude, Li Yan, and Danill fled toward the trucks. The drill started going faster. Magma and liquid metals exploded through the borehole. The NASA team reached the trucks. They drove away from the site. The Department of Defense from Extraterrestrial Contact stayed.

General Summer ordered Brigadier General Hernandez to take down the aircraft. Brigadier General Hernandez commanded the fighter holding the portable surface-to-air missile launcher to fire at the aircraft. Boom. The missile exploded on impact, but nothing happened to Axy's aircraft.

Axy's drill, now in the liquid outer core, continued to burble. A small door opened on the side of Axy's aircraft. A missile exited, bombing the entire Terra Shield unit, including General Summer and Brigadier General Hernandez, and the members of the Department of Defense from Extraterrestrial Contact who had stayed where the trucks were parked. Everyone disintegrated into bubbling pools of blood. Brigadier General Martin Thornton, leading a nearby battalion on standby, ordered a pilot to fire an SM-60 missile, a combined anti-air ballistic weapon, at Axy's aircraft.

Axy had finished drilling through the mantle. The arm of the drill now made quick swishing noises as it went through the liquid outer core. The SM-60 missile hit Axy's aircraft. The weapon slightly dented it on impact.

The arm of the drill lengthened. A loud boom emanated from the center of Earth as the drill bit penetrated the top of the first inner core. The noises from inside Earth now turned to *rat tat tat tat drrrrrr drrrrrr rat tat tat tat drrrrrr drrrrrr* as the drill went through the solid matter of the first inner core. Axy's pilot, who had weapons focused on the enemy's aircraft nearby, fired missiles at two Terra Shield airplanes. They both exploded. Axy's drill continued through the first inner core.

Brigadier General Thornton ordered an advanced artificial intelligence aircraft, using an air-to-air hypersonic nuclear missile that traveled at seven times the speed of sound, to hit Axy's aircraft and the part of its drill above ground. The missile hit its target, creating a hole in Axy's aircraft and slicing through the lower arm of the drill. The bottom part of the drill inside Earth fell down, and the top half remained attached to Axy's aircraft. A large white cloud had formed in the area.

Axy notified its successor on Mars that it was about to press the aircraft's and its own kill switches. Axy landed the aircraft. Brigadier General Thornton ordered Terra Shield's missiles to stop. The humans watched Axy's next step. Axy's copy on Mars confirmed that it was fully awake and ready to take command to complete the mission.

Axy pressed its aircraft's kill switch. The aircraft heated to 15,830 degrees Fahrenheit in five seconds. Then, its alarm system warned that the aircraft would melt in fifteen seconds. Axy activated its own kill switch. Axy heated in five seconds. The airplane and everything in it turned into boiling liquid *irkat*.

www.ingramcontent.com/pod-product-compliance
Ingram Content Group UK Ltd.
Pitfield, Milton Keynes, MK11 3LW, UK
UKHW042037020325
455693UK00008B/29

9 798992 030907